# The New Black Awakening

I0679695

DR. Kasey Yassin Farah

DR. KASEY Y. FARAH

Published by Golis Publishing

4900 Leesburg Pike, Suite 413

Alexandria, VA 22302

Www.golispublishing.com

golismedia@gmail.com

Farah, Kasey Yassin

The New Back Awakening

Fiction Novel

ISBN: 978-0-9907283-7-5

Cover Photo by Yusuf Mohamud Dahir

Cover design:  Farah Mohamed

First edition March 2021

Printed in the United States of America.

# DEDICATION

For my Family

# CONTENTS

## ACKNOWLEDGMENTS

First and foremost, I am grateful to God who makes everything possible. Secondly, I am extremely grateful to my family; my wife Ifrah, my daughters Hoda and Hana and my son Adam who have encouraged me to push forward with writing this book. They have been the cornerstone for the hard work and time that was dedicated to the completion of this book. Many thanks to my friend and experienced writer Mr. Farah Mohamed for being a fierce advocate and valuable supporter for this novel.

# ABOUT THE AUTHOR

Dr. Kasey Y. Farah was born in Somalia and left home when he was a teenager to attend High School in New Jersey, USA. Dr. Farah holds B.S in Health Sciences from Virginia Commonwealth University, and a Doctorate in Dental Surgery from Howard University. He was further trained for Post-Graduate education at the Officer Training School at Newport, Rhode Island and US Naval Medical Center, Bethesda, Maryland as Naval Dental Officer.

Dr. Farah was attached to an amphibious Navy ship as a Department Head and had travelled throughout the world including the Caribbean Sea, Europe, Mediterranean/Middle East, Horn of Africa, and the Persian Gulf.

After being honorably discharged from the United States Navy, Dr. Farah started private practice in Virginia where he lives with his wife and three children.

## DISCLOSURES

This is a work of fiction. Names, characters, places, and incidents either are products of the author's imagination or are used fictitiously. Any resemblance to actual events or locales or persons, living or dead, is entirely coincidental.

## AUTHOR ENGAGEMENT

Dr. Farah is available for select speaking engagements. To inquire about a possible appearance, please contact Golis Publishing at contact@golispublishing.com, or Farah Mohamed at golismedia@gmail.com.

# INTRODUCTION

Dr. Kasey Farah's book, *New Black Awakening*, should be part of every university curriculum in the United States of America—and throughout Africa. Dr. Farah eloquently captures the frustration and fear of young African American professionals who want to leave the United States due to racism and police brutality. He painstakingly stitches together myriad stories of the racism that every Black person in America experiences, including incidents of violence by the police that have been kept out of the headlines.

The story captures of four successful Black professionals in the United States who hail from very different educational, occupational, economical, and familial backgrounds. Each one has prospered in their chosen occupation; however, racism remains the prominent factor in their lives. Reading their stories made me realize that the systematic racism these young professionals face is so deeply engrained in the country's national identity that many Americans cannot admit it exists. However, while racism goes largely unnoticed by those who do not experience it, these stories show that it is alive and well. Many people who have never been the targets of racism and never had police knees on their necks do not understand the psychological damage it inflicts on the souls of generation after generation of African American children, who still grow up knowing and feeling they are second-class citizens in their own country.

My only issue with the book is the solution Dr. Farah proposes. It is heartbreaking that all these young, successful professionals have decided to cut their ties with the country of their birth, as well as with their families and communities. This is particularly discouraging because African Americans have made significant contributions to America's development into a first-world superpower—in fact, many would argue truthfully that the economic and geopolitical dominance of the United States has been achieved on the backs of their enslaved ancestors.

African Americans are uniquely qualified to strengthen the bonds between Africa and the United States. African American professionals possess tremendous assets, and with these they can play a critical role in building a strong and unified Africa. Most African Americans have a general sense of identification with Africa, but no direct connection to any particular African country. As Pan-Africans, they are not Ethiopian, Kenyan, Nigerian, Ghanaian, Senegalese, Somali, or South African, which may liberate them from the ethnic conflict that plagues the continent.

With their wealth of education, experience, and entrepreneurial skills, young African Americans can contribute to their ancestral homeland without abandoning a country that, despite all its shortcomings, has made it possible for them to succeed.

Suleiman S. Ali

# 1

## THE GROUP MEETS

*"If you want to make a political point, write a good book"* **Gabriel García Márquez.**

"So, what's the latest, guys? I have not been keeping up with the current events lately," says Elmer, a partner with a local accounting firm and a practicing certified public accountant for the last twelve years.

Elmer has had a very successful career in high-end corporate accounting. During the busy tax season, he helps his professional friends with their accounting needs. Through word of mouth, many minority business owners have come to Elmer for his accounting advice, and they depend on him to avoid tax overpayment and ensure they follow regulations. He is married and has two teenage boys.

This particular cool Saturday morning, Elmer and his closest friends—Richard, a real estate business owner, Khalid, a physician and former naval officer, and Nikki, a nurse practitioner working at Washington Hospital Center—are having an informal get-together at a local Starbucks in the Washington suburbs of Prince George County, Maryland. They are wearing masks and are practicing the mandated social distancing protocol required by the Maryland Health

Department. This county, which is located a few miles north of Washington, DC, is said to be one of the richest black counties in the country. It sits between the large Washington Metro and Baltimore, nowadays called the DMV or DC. One reason for the affluence of those living in the DMV has to do with the proximity of the federal government, where the largest employer is, indeed, Uncle Sam.

A lot of the affluent African American residents of Prince George's County are employed by the federal government. Some are so well-to-do because of pensions from the military and second careers as consultants, usually with the same Department of Defense they retired from. Another source of income and affluence is the high-tech sector, where information technology, cybersecurity, and consulting firms are on both sides of the Potomac River, including internationally well-known defense contractors, such as Lockheed Martin, McDonnell Douglas, Booz Allen Hamilton, Bae Systems, Raytheon, Northrop Grumman, and General Dynamics. Other sources of well-paying employment are the international organizations headquartered in downtown Washington, DC, such as the World Bank Group, the International Monetary Fund, the WHO branch for the Americas, and the diplomatic missions.

While African-American communities in the DMV are well-to-do compared to other geographic locations in America, even the most affluent professionals are dissatisfied with the way America has been treating its African American citizens. And if the members of such an affluent community are so unhappy with their lives in America, it's easy to imagine how those who live below the poverty line, which could be considered the majority of blacks in America, feel about the situation.

So, these professional African Americans created a discussion group. While the group was initially intended to be a forum to vent to one another about professional issues and the daily hustle and bustle of life, the discussions have turned to more serious probings of what is happening in America and the irony of things getting worse even for those who thought they had achieved the American dream. Just as the average Joe complains about getting pulled over by the police just for being black, doctors, professors, lawyers, and even members of congress are subjugated to the same humiliating treatment: undiscriminating discrimination. Each member of the group has had their unique personal and family experiences of life in America, and these experiences have had a great impact on how each responds to racial situations.

Except for Khalid, who emigrated from East Africa, they were all born in America. The one thing they all have in common, other than race, is that they are all successful professionals. But as they unravel their pasts and the present situation America is in, things will change drastically. Each will have to go back and get reacquainted with their past to explain where they are now and where to go from here as successful professionals, having realized the so-called American dream is no longer enough to be content.

As a young man, Elmer was the type of guy for whom the glass was always half full: upbeat and with not much to worry about, especially when it came to current social conditions. While growing up, his opinion about the bad situation between blacks in America and the police was that if African Americans could just stay out of trouble, then none of these bad outcomes would take place. Of course, that opinion is a rare one among the African American community, but his life experience could have affected his thoughts.

Richard, on the other hand, has had his share of being mistreated by the police and was jailed as a minor. His bad memories have influenced his poor opinion of the police. Nikki probably had the worst experience of all: her stepbrother was killed by a white police officer. The officer was later absolved of any wrongdoing. Khalid, the only one in the group not born in America, has had the least direct interaction with the police, although his son had an almost life-changing collision with law enforcement. To hash out their different experiences, they are going back to where and how it all started.

# 2

# ELMER

*"Justice will not be served until those who are unaffected are as outraged as those who are"*
**Benjamin Franklin**

Elmer was raised by a white upper-middle-class suburban couple: Frank Wilson and his wife, Karen, who adopted him after his biological mother died at birth. His biological father was a Haitian immigrant, but Elmer only knew him for a short time, as he was deported when Elmer was six. His father did not want to lose him, but as an illegal immigrant, he could not keep his child. As his deportation proceedings got closer, he had only one option: to give up Elmer for adoption. So, the state gave full legal custody of Elmer to a rich white couple.

Elmer had a great life; he was part of the affluent community of Annapolis, the capital of Maryland and the location of the elite United

States Naval Academy. Elmer's adoptive father was an international arms dealer with great connections to the Department of Defense and the American military-industrial complex. Elmer's father traveled widely, to the Middle East and the former Soviet Union countries, to make defense equipment deals and purchases. Elmer's mother held a prominent position in the National Rifle Association, headquartered in Fairfax, Virginia. They were both well-known political donors to the Republican Party as well as Maryland delegates for Republican National Convention conferences.

The couple did not have their own biological children, and Elmer was everything to them. Because of their insecurity, they did everything they could to cut off the relationship between Elmer and his biological father. Although Elmer's biological father was far away in Haiti, he always tried to write to his son and keep the line of communication open. However, Elmer's adoptive parents, especially his mom, would shred the letters so Elmer never received them. Special occasions, such as birthdays and other annual holidays, were especially painful for the young boy, as he expected to hear from his biological father.

The couple raised Elmer just like one of the kids in their rich white neighborhood. As some adoptive parents of ethnic children try to do, this couple did everything they could to instill their biological identity and culture in the child, confusing him greatly. One of the most painful experiences Elmer had to face as a young boy was when one of his classmates had a birthday party. The party invitations went to every boy and girl in class but Elmer. At school Monday morning, the kids talked about nothing but how great the party was. When Elmer asked his classmate why he was not invited, the classmate told him that it was because he was black and his parents had told him that black people were not good. This experience was very painful for Elmer's young mind. When Elmer shared this information with his adoptive mom, she told him that it was just a joke and the kid was only teasing him and that Elmer should not worry too much about it.

Elmer went to one of the best private schools in the area. He was on the basketball team and did so well that he was almost recruited as a future NBA star. However, his adoptive parents did not want him to pursue such a career. They were of the opinion that Elmer was too good to be among guys who run around with bouncing balls, whose main existence in life is to entertain others. They wanted him to go to a great college and get connections from his father's friends.

It appeared as though Elmer's adoptive parents were concerned about every aspect of his life except for his emotional well-being. While they might have been raising a successful child materially, they were also raising a confused young adult. Except for the color of his skin, Elmer could be identified as a white boy in every aspect of his life. To his credit, he tried to locate his biological father. You see, blood is thicker than water, and as Elmer grew older and wiser, he realized that identity is crucial and, even if he and his father did not understand each other culturally or otherwise, they should be able to communicate.

Elmer was very wise for his young age; somehow, deep in his psyche, he knew that his father had not abandoned him, although his adoptive mother tried hard to make Elmer think that way. As he grew older, he tried to even travel to cities where Haitian communities were concentrated, such as Miami, Washington, DC, and the Bronx side of New York. With only the first and last name of his father to go by, it was next to impossible to locate his father's connections, if there were even any in the United States. Unfortunately, Elmer had no success at all. Luckily, though, the seed of curiosity to find out his true identity was sown.

After graduating from high school with excellent grades, Elmer went to college and attended the very prestigious Johns Hopkins University, in Baltimore. He chose the major of accounting and finance. This was an idea from his father, who had been a trained accountant and chief CPA with Deloitte and Touche for over twenty years. He wanted Elmer to get his CPA and be employed by one of the top accounting firms in America.

Elmer's adoptive mother had a different opinion. She had the wrong idea about Baltimore, that it was a rundown city with crimes and drugs. She did not want Elmer to go there; she preferred that he go to Penn State, where she had gone, or Georgetown, which would be close enough for him to come home every weekend. It appeared that she did not want Elmer to leave the nest, at least not too far. Nor did she want him to broaden his scope. Why would he need to do so anyway? If he needed money, he had it through their family wealth. After a long debate, Elmer and his father won the argument.

Elmer was well prepared for the task at hand and got along well with college life. As they say, one finds oneself during those formative college years, and Elmer was no exception. He had only good things to say about his life with his adoptive parents, but the one thing he had no opportunity for was to get to know who he really was. Going to an all-white private school and living in a Caucasian, upper-class neighborhood did not get him ready for the real world out there.

Elmer tried to participate in all kinds of Afrocentric clubs at Johns Hopkins and the wider Baltimore black community. He became a member of the United Africa Club, where lectures and meetings about mother Africa and how the African diaspora could connect the two sides of the Atlantic were held. He was fascinated by Haitian history and how the French colonizers were defeated by the Haitian liberators led by Francois-Dominique Toussaint Louverture. General Toussaint helped eliminate the use of race as the basis for social ranking.

Elmer was taken aback that he was never taught about this side of his identity. He was shocked that with all the books his parents had made him read about the history of European civilization, there had

17

not been a single pamphlet about the history of the black people and African culture. It was like he was learning a new subject altogether, one he wanted to learn quickly and voluminously. He could not wait until the next meeting or lecture series about Africa and African culture. He took so many courses that had nothing to do with accounting and were not required by the School of Business.

One night, Elmer was having a long discussion with one of the African Club leaders, who suggested that Elmer take African studies as a minor, especially with all the credit hours he had accumulated. Elmer thought that was such a great idea. He participated in a touring club that took African studies majors to West Africa to explore African culture. Elmer wanted to see the landmarks of Ghana, Senegal, and The Gambia, where the slave ships had sailed from and mothers, fathers, and children had been taken away against their will to a land they knew nothing about.

This was Elmer's junior year in college, and he wanted the experience of travel. His adoptive father always bragged about traveling to many continents, and though he wanted Elmer to do the same, this plan to travel to West Africa was not the traveling that he'd had in mind. The trip was to coincide with spring break, and Elmer had the means to arrange and plan the trip with his friends and classmates at the Department of African Studies. He already had his American Express Platinum with no limits on it; all he had to do was apply for an expedited American passport.

Three weeks before his departure date, he came home to Annapolis for the weekend. His parents missed him. You see, before Elmer got involved with the African Club and activities related to Afrocentric awareness, he had always come home every Friday afternoon. With Annapolis a stone's throw from Baltimore, he would drive his convertible home and spend the weekend at his parents' waterfront property. There, Elmer would spend time with his old friends and parents. As they grew older, seeing Elmer and catching up with him on school matters became very important, and they always looked forward to him returning home and spending the weekend with them.

However, things changed dramatically for Elmer as he got involved with his new African identity. Rather than hanging out with previous friends of similar socioeconomic status, Elmer now valued the new friends he had made in Baltimore. He'd suddenly found himself, and he wished he had gone to Morgan State or Howard University rather than Johns Hopkins. He was more interested in African history than preparing for the CPA (certified public accountant) exam. His weekends were spent with his Baltimore friends instead of coming home. Since school organizations plan their social functions on the weekends to avoid conflict with academic obligations on weekdays, Elmer had to stay in Baltimore most of his weekends. Furthermore, he found himself enjoying spending time there and participating in those functions. It was almost like a religious duty.

His parents were becoming concerned with the situation. They did not understand why Elmer would not come home on the weekends. They even wondered if he might have met a new girlfriend. But if so, why would he not introduce her to them? They certainly would want to meet her. On a more negative thought, his mother thought that Elmer might have gotten involved with the wrong crowd. With the negative perception she had about Baltimore, she worried that her son might be up to no good. She started to blame her husband for encouraging Elmer to go to college in Baltimore in the first place.

One day, Elmer's mother picked up a package from the UPS delivery man. It was addressed to him. She freaked out, thinking that the package was from his biological father. She had made a concentrated effort to keep Elmer from his biological father, but her husband, on the other hand, understood the value of identity and the importance of kinship and bloodline. His parents were holocaust survivors who had lost their parents and siblings in the concentration camps of Nazi-occupied Poland. He understood the difference between adoption and biological relationship. He believed that Elmer should reconnect with his father on his own terms and that connection should never be hindered or obstructed.

As she opened the package, she found something almost as shocking: a newly ordered and expedited passport from the State Department. She wondered why and where Elmer was going and why he hadn't told them. It added to her paranoia about Elmer not coming home on the weekends and not as often. Answering herself, she thought that since spring break was fast approaching, perhaps he was planning a trip to France or Spain with his Mediterranean-loving friends. Little did she know that Elmer was planning to cross a different part of the Atlantic.

Elmer came home to check if the passport had arrived; he had been checking the delivery status all along to make sure he got the visa stamps through his college's Department of African Studies, which was organizing the Africa trip.

His parents had planned an elaborate dinner that night to celebrate his homecoming after a long hiatus. His mother was not in her joyous mood that evening and kept asking Elmer what was happening with him and why he had not been coming home lately. He told her that he was getting ready for the CPA exam and that he had added an additional minor to his accounting major. His mother wanted to know which one, finance or marketing.

Elmer knew she would find the answer highly unexpected, but he told her that he was taking African studies as a minor and that he had been exploring the field of African history and culture. His father, at the head of the table joked, "Oh, it looks like Elmer is making up for the lost time." Elmer's adoptive mother was not amused; she asked him what the benefit was of spending time and effort on history that anyone could read in a history book. This struck a nerve with Elmer; he'd never had the opportunity to read a history book about Africa because his family did not value that type of history. But he was a very respectful young man, not one to raise his voice to his mother at the dinner table, no matter how distasteful her comment was to him.

She continued her interrogation about his newly arrived passport. Elmer was offended that she would open his package. He did not say anything, but she noticed the expression on his face. She apologized for opening it, using the excuse that she'd thought it was hers as she had been expecting a package and had opened it without reading the name. She said that it would be a great idea if the three of them took a trip to the French Riviera on Elmer's spring break, especially now that Elmer has his passport.

At that point, Elmer was emboldened to put it all out there. He told his family that he had been on a mission to find out who he really was, his identity. He reminded his mom about that childhood experience when his classmate had not invited him to his party because his family had told him that blacks were no good. Elmer told his parents that everything had come back to him when he'd started college and met people who looked like him. He told his parents that he had been lying to himself all these years. That while they provided him a lot of love and material things, he lacked the most important aspect of a young man's life: his Identity and sense of belonging. His father started to weep, as he knew that it had never been his idea and he had always disagreed with his wife about this particular subject.

Elmer told it like it was. He was not going to hide the fact that he was beginning to embrace his true identity, that he was going to West Africa as part of a pilgrimage with students and faculty members from Morgan State University and Johns Hopkins, and that they were touring the slave trade routes of Ghana, Senegal, and The Gambia. He told them this was a bi-annual visit in which the Department of African Studies sponsored trips to conduct research and for continuing education. He told his parents that he'd ordered the passport and would be leaving in a matter of weeks.

His mother was very worried about his safety and did not understand why anyone would want to research what had happened four hundred years ago. As usual, her husband had to correct her by saying, "Four hundred years is just yesterday, honey. Egyptologists study things from thousands of years ago."

She rolled her eyes, as she never liked to be outsmarted. Seeing how serious Elmer was about the visit, she told him to make sure to see Dr. Sugarman, their family physician, to get malaria medicine. She also pointed out to him to stay safe. "You know, they have AIDs over there."

Elmer replied, "They have more aids in Baltimore than where I am going." Again, she was not amused, but she got the point. Elmer was a different kind of son now, assertive and not shy about respectfully standing up to her.

After dinner, Elmer went up to his part of the house and tried to unwind. Downstairs, his parents continued to talk about his unexpected transformation, how he had become a different person. Elmer's adopted father always wanted to support his son, but he wanted Elmer to lead his own life. Whether Elmer wanted to search for his biological family or not, his father was going to be by his side. However, the wife was completely obsessed with Elmer. It was like she did not want him to move on with his life. The two always had heated arguments on the subject.

Elmer went with the tour group to Africa. They landed in Accra, the capital of Ghana, and were received by highly ranked officials from the University of Ghana, which was hosting the tour. It was midmorning Africa time, and the American group was a bit jetlagged. After a hearty late breakfast at the Accra Intercontinental Hotel, the guests were let go for rest. Elmer was the only student who had never been to Africa. He was not in the mood to sleep. He wanted to take it all in. He had never seen a place with so many black people. Every turn he made, he saw a black face like his. For the first time in his life, Elmer felt he was home. Even Baltimore, with its sizeable number of blacks, did not seem remotely close. He took a shower, changed, and started walking the streets of Accra. Interestingly, people noticed that he was not from there, but they were very polite and told him, "Welcome home, brother." It appeared they'd read his face and seen his enthusiastic curiosity.

After many hours, Elmer came back to the hotel to get ready for the evening's agenda. The plan was to dine with members of the African studies department of the University of Ghana. The department chair went over the agenda. The venue was one of the best restaurants on the beach of Accra, with a great view of the sunset over the Atlantic. Everyone had a great time conversing and getting to know one another. One of the conveniences of being in Ghana was that English is widely spoken there; therefore, there was no language barrier. Unlike some Francophone African countries where French is spoken, such as Senegal, Cameroon, and Mali, Ghana was an English colony.

Elmer had already learned about this important country, not only its history as one of the slave coasts of West Africa but also how instrumental Ghana was for the Pan-Africanism movement of the 1960s. This movement, led by prominent Africans such as Kwame Nkrumah, the first president of Ghana, Patrice Lumumba of the Republic of Congo, W.E.B. Du Bois of the US, Julius Nyerere of Tanzania, Marcus Garvey, and other African, African Americans, and Caribbean leaders, tried to unite the people of African descent, if not through geographic proximity, at least through political freedom and equality within their respective locations.

For the first time, Elmer saw with his own eyes historical locations and monuments that he'd only read about in texts on African history back in Baltimore. How peaceful and content communities of mothers, daughters, brothers, and even elderly men and women were snatched in the dead of night, abducted against their will. How they were all blindfolded and treated worse than cattle, herded into empty, dark spaces with no windows and air to breathe. How they were shackled together by the ankle and were numbered rather than named by their God-given identity. How they were all crammed into the bottoms of ships, still confused, cold, and hungry. How many of them died on the journey to an unknown and forsaken place and were then thrown overboard.

Elmer had begun to regret his life with his adoptive parents. He found that part of his life a lie, and he felt unforgiving toward his adoptive mother. Why would she hide so much from him? But at the same time, he blamed himself for not searching for his true self. He blamed himself for not reading about his background. He knew he was not white; the color of his skin was a testament to that. But even if he decided not to look in the mirror that often, his elementary school classmate had made that point apparent to him.

*As they say, better late than never*, thought Elmer. He was still a young man, and he had a lot of time ahead of him. He thought about ways to redeem himself, to make up for the lost time, to reconnect with the dormant roots that could be dying but were still salvageable, to find his true family, his biological family, a tree that was half dead but half alive. Elmer put all his energy to get deep into the Haitian-American community, to find out how he could locate any kin or kith who could help him find his father.

After dinner, the tour program coordinator, a PhD candidate from the University of Ghana, Mr. Kwashe Asande, went over the details of the next day's tour agenda. This included a visit to Cape Coast Castle. As explained by Mr. Asande, this was one of the largest commercial forts built by white slave traders on the Gold Coast, what is now the country of Ghana. As a Portuguese trading post, it was established in 1555. The Portuguese were replaced by the Swedish Timber Company in 1653. The Swedes also traded gold there.

At hearing this, Elmer could not help but lament how Europeans enriched themselves with African resources. He remembered one of the assigned books for his African history class titled *How Europe Underdeveloped Africa*, by Walter Rodney. In one place out of many, Elmer was going to come face to face with how Africa was not only robbed of its human resources, but also its natural resources, such as timber, gold, silver, ivory, rubber, and much more.

The other places slated for a tour the next day included Elmina Castle and Fort Christiansborg. Both of these castles were places where the African slaves were shipped to the Americas to be sold. The guests from the US, including Elmer, were given a good night wish and were instructed to meet at 7:30 am in the hotel lobby for breakfast and then told to be ready for the bus tour by no later than 8:15 in front of the hotel. Elmer went up to his room and went to sleep. He was very keen about recording as much history as possible. He'd already promised himself that this was something he would have to share with his future children, a history lesson that must be taught to every African American kid.

The next morning, Elmer was eager to embark on this journey of history and search for identity. He had his phone ready to tape every detail provided by the tour guide. They arrived at the Cape Coast Castle. As described by the tour guide, the Swedish Africa Company built the castle to steal African gold and timber for international markets. The company was founded by Louis De Geer in 1649.

The Cape Coast Castle later became a trans-Atlantic slave-trading post. The castle had multiple locations for holding the slaves before they were moved into transatlantic ships. The tour guide explained how terrible the conditions of the castle were. In the underground dungeon were spaces of terror, death, and darkness. In this dark and godforsaken basement of hell, the slaves usually urinated, slept, and sometimes died on the same cold cement floor. For those who were unlucky enough not to die in it, it was the last place in their memory of their homeland. Many among the touring party just could not handle the whole thing and started to weep; one commented how strong her ancestors were, for she was a true attestation of their strength as she was right there to see what happened over four hundred years ago. She made the point that she was proud of the grit of her forefathers, but ashamed of the weakness of those humans who thought that what they did to Africans centuries ago made them strong, and unfortunately, many still feel that way to this day.

After the completion of that emotional tour at the Cape Coast Castle, the group enjoyed an elaborate luncheon on the deck of a hotel on the beach, hosted by the director-general of the Ministry of Education of Ghana. The program was to welcome the guests from America and thank them for their interest in Ghana.

After a brief introduction by Mr. Asande, the director started his speech. "Ladies and gentlemen, it is with my honor and pleasure to welcome you not only as guests, but more importantly, as brothers and sisters. I am very pleased to welcome you all to your homeland, your kinship, your sand, and your soil. We might have the mighty Atlantic Ocean between us, but indeed, we are much closer than the waves of the water you now see. I particularly am fond of America and Americans. You see, not long ago, I was like you, a student at one of the most prestigious universities of America, the one and only University Of Virginia. I loved the mountains of Charlottesville, the greenery of Albemarle and Greene Counties, and the hills and farmland of Madison County. But most importantly, I loved the products of your ancestors' blood and sweat in the plantations of Southern Virginia.

"While I cherished my years in Virginia, it is also poignantly imperative to point out that it was Virginia where the first slave ships that left these waters arrived. But as they say, in every darkness, there's a light. In every struggle, there's a way. In every faith, there's a hope. You, ladies and gentlemen, are the light of the darkness of slavery. America must know that it would not be as developed, prosperous, cultured, and vibrantly colored without the minds, the muscle, the might, the music, the faith, and the determination of Africans. It would be dull and cold, lame and lusterless, faint and feeble, weak and wobbly.

"Now, it is not entirely unexpected for humans to be forgetful of lessons of yesterday. America might have forgotten who built it, its agriculture, its highways, its capitals, its railroad systems. It was not the Polish, who came from 1820 and 1914. It was not the Portuguese in the 1870s. It was not the Italians, who came from 1880 to the 1920s. It was the slaves and their descendants. You must understand, if you don't learn about your own history, the current majority educational system will not teach you that. They want you to forget about your true history. They want you to think that you are lucky to have been brought to America, and if you don't know the facts, if you don't know your history, someone else will teach you their version of it.

"If I may borrow the true words of one of the well-known leaders of colonial Europe, Jacques Rene Chirac, the president of France, to be exact, he said, and I quote, 'WE BLED AFRICA FOR FOUR AND A HALF CENTURIES. We looted their raw materials, and then we told lies that the Africans are good for nothing. In the name of religion, we destroyed their culture. And after being made rich at their expense, we now steal their brains through miseducation and propaganda to prevent them from enacting black retribution against us.' That sums up the crimes against Africa by the West.

"What you are doing by visiting these sites is remarkable. It is a homage to your ancestors, those who made it safely to the other side of the Atlantic as well as those who perished, may God rest their souls. I want to tell you that there is a trend going on, one that I never thought I would live to see. There is reverse migration of African Americans back home. I can personally attest to that as former American collegemates and friends have moved to Ghana and The Gambia to live and start new businesses. Everyone I know who moved here from America has told me why they couldn't think of this years back.

"This is not a lecture for me to proselytize you all to pack your bags all at once and leave your homeland – but wait a minute. This is your true home, and I don't have to convince you that it is your home. Can anyone tell me that they at the least did not feel some type of emotional goosebumps when they arrived in Africa? That tells you that you have come home. Africa is large enough for the entire African-American population. Africa is vast in its resources, natural and otherwise. It is ripe for infrastructure investment. It is the new frontier. We want you to come home, to share with us the God-given resources before the Chinese get here. I wish all of you a pleasant stay in your homeland. May God almighty bless you and our ancestors."

That speech left Elmer with huge mixed feelings; his emotional sense of belonging to this place the first time he landed in Accra, coupled with that heartfelt speech, created the ease with which his future quest for identity search would be initiated, and with high speed. That afternoon, the group set out for the second tour of the day to see the Elmina Castle.

The Castle was located in a coastal area of Ghana called Elmina, from which it derived its name. As described by the curator of the building, the people who inhabited Elmina in the fifteenth century were the Fante tribe. This tribe was concentrated in the center of Ghana as well as the Ivory Coast. Living near the coastline of Ghana allowed the Fante and their neighboring tribes to trade their mined gold with the Mediterranean and Near East. In addition to gold mining, there was a great deal of forest timber, which contributed to the construction and infrastructure developments of European countries.

To draw some perspective for the young American students, the tour guide identified some well-know international figures who belonged to the Fante tribe: Kofi Annan, the former secretary general of the United Nations, Peter Turkson, Ghanaian cardinal of the Catholic Church and former president of the Pontifical Council for Justice and Peace, John Atta Mills, former president of Ghana, and many others.

The Elmina Castle was built by the Portuguese in the late 1400s. As the oldest trading post on the Gulf of Guinea, it later became one of the stops for the Atlantic slave trade. It was later occupied by the Dutch in 1637, which continued the slave trade until 1814. As it changed European hands based on the geopolitical changes at the time, the Dutch lost the area to the British in 1872.

To mix the touring milieu, the tour guide suggested that for their next adventure, the group visit Kwame Nkrumah Memorial Park. Although the late Ghanaian president was well known among the American touring students, the guide did not spare anything to describe the person all Ghanaians believe to be a hero. The memorial park is located in the center of Accra. The final resting place of the late leader is a huge attraction.

As the end of the visit to the Gold Coast of Africa got closer, Elmer was filled with a huge sense of accomplishment. He felt that he had planted the deep seeds to go forward. The last day before his return home, Elmer took a long walk along the coast of the Atlantic Ocean. In his head, he played the unimaginable scenario where human beings were sold and shipped across those blue waters to unknown lands, sold and resold again, and thought about how his ancestors were shipped to the Caribbean and the sugar plantations of Haiti.

Elmer and his friends left Ghana. The route back home was by way of Addis Ababa, Ethiopia, where they had a ten-hour flight connection to Washington. They all planned to make the most of their time there and explore the city. Elmer had the opportunity to see one of the oldest cities in sub-Saharan Africa. He studied the history of Ethiopia and the role it played in fighting the Italian invasion. The battle of Adwa was well presented at one of the most revered museums in Addis Ababa. There, the historian introduced a short history lesson for Elmer and his American friends.

As presented by the narrator, the Battle of Adwa was instrumental in ensuring Ethiopia's position as Africa's only country that was never colonized. Winning this battle prevented the expansion of the Italian imperialists into the rest of Africa. It was also somewhat of an impetus for the Pan-Africanism movement and the eventual creation of the Organization of African Unity. At the battle of Adwa, the Ethiopians outnumbered the Italians, who never thought in their wildest dreams that a poor black country with a backward army and no navy or air force would expel them, defeated and fending for their lives. Such an empty, pejorative opinion of Africans by the Italians led to the biggest embarrassment in the history of warfare. In other words, the white Italians really underestimated the power of the thirst for dying with dignity. After leaving Addis Ababa, Elmer promised to return.

Elmer came back home and was picked up from the Dulles International Airport by one of his best friends from high school. His friend, Jim, wanted to know how his trip was. Elmer told him that it was great and he would highly recommend it. He came home to find his parents eagerly waiting. His mother showed a visible sense of relief that he was back home, like the mother of a Marine son who has been gone to a war zone would feel after he has returned. Elmer was keenly aware of her state of being, but he did not share the sentiment. In fact, it increased his sense of bitterness about how she had always prevented him from learning about his roots. His father was happy to see him, too, but without the unnecessary emotional futility.

Elmer was invited to a lunch his mother had prepared for his arrival, perhaps thinking that Elmer must have starved while in Africa or might have missed the American food he was accustomed to. Little did she know that genes are stronger than the palate and Elmer had had a great time eating the dishes served in West Africa, such as fufuo, banku, or jollof rice, and the East African foods like enjera, tibs, and kifto. Elmer did not like how condescending his mother was being about the culture and cuisines of Africa and his trip there, but he was always deferential to her and had to bite his tongue. At the dining table, his father tried to change the subject, knowing that his wife would offend Elmer and Elmer could only be patient for so long.

After lunch, Elmer decided to take a nap and recover from his jetlag. His parents planned to have him join them on their weekend yacht on the Chesapeake Bay. They had invited their friends as well. When Elmer woke up around 5:00 pm on Friday, his mother told him that she wanted him to get ready for the trip so he could unwind on the yacht and enjoy his return to the civilized world. That was the straw that broke the camel's back. Elmer just lost it, and he told his mother that the most uncivilized people on the face of the earth were those who traded and enslaved human beings to do what they could not do. "The so-called civilized world is built on the backs of those you are calling uncivilized."

Elmer did not wait for any further discussion; he left home at once and went to his friend's apartment in Baltimore. He refused to answer phone calls from his parents until the next morning. They had to cancel the trip to the bay to resolve the issues with Elmer.

While in Baltimore, Elmer had a long discussion with his friend Louis, who was a graduate student at Morgan State, finalizing his thesis on African-American repatriation to the homeland. Elmer shared with Louis his conflict with his adopted mother and how she was so bent on cutting him from his true identity. Louis was well aware of how some white families who adopt minority children tend to confuse them, but the truth eventually sets everyone free.

Late Saturday evening, Elmer decided to go home and pick up the few gifts he'd brought for his friends. He came into the house while his parents were out. He went up to his room and read some of the books he'd brought from Africa. His parents came back, and his father went upstairs to shower while his mother went through the mail. She was notorious for always being the first to pick up the mail. His father came down to the family room to watch the evening news as his mother was busy shredding paper in the home office. Then the old man went over to her and asked her what she was trying to shred. The couple started yelling and screaming at each other. They did not realize that Elmer was in the house.

Initially, Elmer thought the argument over the shredded letters had to do with those secret weapon sales his father was involved in and that his mother might have mistakenly destroyed some documents. As they continued to argue, the father yelled, "Why in hell would you want the boy and his biological father not to connect? They need each other. Sooner or later, Elmer will find where his father is, and it is only right that we facilitate that relationship. Whether they succeed in finding each other or not is not up to us, but we can't destroy it before it starts." After a pause, Elmer's father continued to plead with his wife. "Would you be happy if your lost child tried to locate you and their adoptive parents shredded the letters?"

That is when it became apparent to Elmer that his mother had been trying all along to prevent the reunification of Elmer and his biological father. Now the ball was in Elmer's court. Should he confront his mother about this, should he secretively deal with his adoptive father to facilitate the connection, if he even had any idea how, or should he cut off his mother altogether and force her to confess under pressure? All these ideas hit him like a brick at once. He decided to play dumb and avoid bringing up the issue until he could consult with some of his friends and come up with a game plan.

The next morning, he woke up normally and had breakfast. His parents must have thought that he'd come in late from an evening in town. His demeanor at the breakfast table did not portray anything out of the ordinary. He told them goodbye as he headed out for Baltimore with his friends.

Elmer's friends gave him different suggestions as to how to deal with the issue of locating his biological father. Some told him to confront his mother and let her come clean. Obviously, she had been receiving letters from him, and she knew his address in Port-au-Prince, Haiti. If she cared about Elmer so much, why would she not care about his quest to locate his father? Others did not want to give that much importance to her; they thought that if she had any heart, she would not have done the evil thing of destroying letters from a loving father to his lost son. They suggested that Elmer do his investigation on his own, using what he'd discovered so far, and perhaps, since the Haitian community in the US is very closely knit, someone might find someone who knew someone.

Elmer had a choice to make. He was leaning towards the idea of doing it on his own. He decided that after the spring, when he completed classes for the semester and passed his CPA test, he would start his quest to find his biological father or anyone who knew him in America.

He started with phone calls to the Haitian community centers in Washington, New York, and Miami. In Washington, nothing came up at all. Most of the Haitians there were former diplomats of different Haitian governments that were either overthrown or lost power. They were the elites, and his father, an illegal immigrant who was subsequently deported, would not be among them.

Elmer switched his search to New York City. That was more of a local place for many Caribbean immigrants, including Dominicans, Haitians, and Jamaicans. He was able to get some good leads, people who knew other people. One of the key reasons it was very difficult for Elmer to pinpoint the identity of his biological father was the wrong information he had been given by his adoptive mother about his biological parents – more specifically, the full name of his biological father. He knew that his mother had died right after he was born; however, he had been wrongly informed that his father's full name was Louis Pierre.

He didn't know when and how his biological father happened to come to the United States. According to his adoptive mother, Louis Pierre was one of those Haitians who came on the boats by way of Cuba in the early 1970s. She said that Louis met Elmer's mother in the Washington area.

Elmer told the Haitian immigrants he contacted in New York that his father's name was Louise Pierre and that he might have come to America in the early 1970s. Elmer was given the name of a Haitian gentleman who was chairman of the Washington, DC, Haitian community at that time. His name was Mr. Antonio Estima. He was residing in Miami. Elmer was able to call him and explain his situation.

Mr. Estima knew who was who among the Haitians in DC of the 1970s. He was a foreign student at the American University School of Foreign Service during the Haitian presidency of Paul Eugene Magloire, who governed from 1950to 1956. Mr. Estima was being groomed to be the ambassador of Haiti in Washington after receiving his PhD in diplomatic relations from AU.

He lamented to Elmer that right after he defended his dissertation in 1956, President Magloire was overthrown. Everything went out the window. Mr. Estima had one of two choices: go back to Haiti and face an uncertain future, to put it mildly, or apply for a teaching assistant position at the university where he'd received his PhD. Dr. Estima said that he had to put his pride aside and settle for the teaching assistant position. It was humiliating, but it was the safe thing to do.

Dr. Estima said, "From almost being an ambassador to working as a teaching assistant, my situation could not have gotten any lower." A wise man, Dr. Estima told the young Elmer, "Life will never be what you plan it to be. You have to do the best you can to deal with what obstacles life presents you with." He told Elmer that after years of struggle as a low-paid American university employee, he was finally offered an assistant professor position, where he taught till his retirement. He was never able to go back to Haiti, as he was viewed as being too close to the overthrown regime.

Elmer told Dr. Estima how he was trying to locate his father, who had been deported back to Haiti. Dr. Estima was not able to recall anyone by the name of Louis Pierre, but he said that he was still in contact with several former workers of the Haitian Cultural Center in Washington and he would probe this further. They exchanged addresses, and Elmer made sure that he gave the old man a postal box number to which any correspondence could be addressed.

Elmer took his final exams and passed his CPA exam. He now only had a year before graduation and getting ready to be a public accountant. He spent most of his time in Baltimore, where he started networking and looking for ways to ensure employment after graduation. He was not keen about depending on his father for connections, as was initially planned. He wanted to show them that he would do things his way. Fortunately, his adoptive father was very understanding of that, unlike his mother.

Elmer checked his mailbox in Baltimore's downtown post office on a weekly basis, hoping to find a letter or something from Dr. Estima. On one cool fall day, he went for a jog in the city. It was early October, and the leaves on the beautiful Baltimore trees had already turned dark gold. After completing a great cardio run, Elmer went to the post office to check his box. There was a letter from Miami. Dr. Estima was an old-fashioned letter writer. As part of his diplomatic training, he'd learned that you type a cable, not hand-write it, lest the recipient incorrectly interpret the contents. Even the envelope was typewritten.

After cordial greetings and well wishes, Dr. Estima broke the news Elmer had been hoping for. Dr. Estima had discovered the identity of Elmer's true father, whose real, full name was Louis Pierre Pascal. Elmer's father was not a stowaway on a boat from Cuba, as described by his adoptive mother. His father was not the illiterate, ignorant man he was portrayed as. Dr. Estima told Elmer that the best way to digest all this information, and much more, would be to meet him in person and to be prepared for a long, perhaps painful conversation, though it would be as truthful as Elmer would want. Dr. Estima closed the letter by telling Elmer that he was welcome as a guest in his home while in Miami.

Elmer arranged a flight to Miami to meet Dr. Estima at his home, and he informed his father that he was flying to Miami to meet some prospective employers there and to see if it would be a city where he would be interested in living. Elmer arrived at Dr. Estima's house on a Friday evening, around 5:00 pm, for dinner with Dr. Estima and his wife, Carolina. After a great Mexican dinner, Mrs. Estima left the two men on their own to unravel the mystery.

Dr. Estima was a very intelligent man, very aware of human emotions as part of his training as a diplomat. He told Elmer that what he was about to hear could be very upsetting; it could create both immediate pain as well as future discomfort. If the end game was for Elmer to locate his biological father, it was within reach, but the road would be difficult. Elmer told Dr. Estima that no pain in the world would stop him from reaching that end.

Dr. Estima started with a prayer to make everything at ease for both of them. He told Elmer, as before, that his father's last name was Pascal. Elmer's father was one of the clerks who worked at the office of the Haitian cultural attaché. He was there from 1968 to late 1971. After the takeover of Jean-Claud Duvalier, there was a big change in the diplomatic corps; a lot of mid-level diplomats who were called back were arrested, and some became fearful of going back to Haiti voluntarily. Dr. Estima informed Elmer that his father could not go back for fear of persecution. He spent some time living on his savings, but when those funds ran out, he was employed as a chauffeur by a wealthy accountant, a Mr. Wilson, who owned an international defense company, a euphemism for an international arms dealer. Dr. Estima acknowledged that while he did not know Mr. Pascal on a personal level, he knew of him and his situation, as the Haitian community was very caring for each other.

Dr. Estima went on to say that as time went by, Mr. Pascal almost became a live-in driver for the family. He assisted the wife, Mrs. Wilson, with her daily errands and drove her to various social events. As time went by, Mr. Wilson got into arms dealing internationally, and that led him to travel to Africa, Latin America, and the Middle East, everywhere that American weaponry was needed and wherever America was selling arms to fatten up its military-industrial complex.

So, Mrs. Wilson would have Mr. Pascal help her with gardening the sprawling, ten-acre waterfront estate in Annapolis. Mr. Pascal was known among his community and colleagues at the Haitian embassy as a very kind, calm, and collected man who cared about people and their feelings. He had been due for a promotion before the changes in Port-au-Prince.

As Mr. Wilson's international travels increased with the demands for arms around the globe, especially American-made, he was gone more than he was in the US. Mrs. Wilson needed a man to help her in the house; that man also needed a job he could not get legally, as he was neither a legal immigrant nor a diplomat as before. He was forced to work for his life. Mrs. Wilson took advantage of that predicament. She knew that he was illegal and could not get a job from the embassy due to the changes in government, and that even his return to Haiti would put his life in danger. Mrs. Wilson asked Mr. Pascal to move into the house while her husband was gone. Mr. Pascal was not shocked because of other previous approaches that Mrs. Wilson had made towards him that went beyond assisting in the garden. Those approaches had to do with different types of gardening.

As a diplomat, Dr. Estima was being very professional. He told Elmer that this was going to be a tough discussion and if Elmer ever wanted him to stop or take a break, it would be no problem. Elmer gave him permission to continue, so Dr. Estima went on.

So, there was a fork in the road for Mr. Pascal: refuse to move in and risk being jobless or get deported, as she could report him to the Immigration and Naturalization Service. He reluctantly moved in. The Wilsons lived on a huge estate with private entrances, and the neighbors and friends had no clue that a man lived in the house when Mr. Wilson was gone. If she had a party with guests over, Mr. Pascal was only among the helpers. To leave the rest to the imagination, Mr. Pascal lived in the master suite while he was there, and sometimes Mr. Wilson was away for months. As Mrs. Wilson had been told a decade ago that she could never have children, the issue of accidental pregnancy with Mr. Pascal was out of the picture.

This went on for years. As fate would have it, Mr. Pascal was in love with a young Haitian homemaker who was herself among the undocumented immigrants who had come to America during the civil unrest in Haiti. Mr. Pascal was torn between what he wanted to do and what he was forced to do. Initially, Mr. Pascal had things under control; he would stay at the Wilsons' estate when the gentleman of the house was on business trips; when Mr. Wilson was in town, Mr. Pascal stayed at his shared apartment with friends in downtown Washington.

Gradually, Mr. Pascal's relationship with his Haitian girlfriend grew more serious. The couple planned to get married; Mr. Pascal, however, was cautious and wanted to keep things quiet to keep Mrs. Wilson from finding out. His girlfriend, who, at this juncture, was suspicious as to what was holding up progress with her future husband, wanted to get a final answer. Mr. Pascal had to make a choice.

A few months after he was given the ultimatum, his girlfriend called for an urgent meeting. He thought that it would be bad news, that she was going to break up with him since he was unable to make a decision on their future. She must have been very upset that he had not been with her for close to four weeks now, and he could not figure out what the emergency was about. Mr. Wilson was gone for four weeks on a trip to Poland and the Balkans for an arms sale conference. Mr. Pascal could never tell his girlfriend about the predicament he was in, nor could he tell Mrs. Wilson about his new relationship. He was between a rock and a hard place.

He went ahead with the meeting, ready for a showdown. She told him that she was two months pregnant and had been very sick during the pregnancy. She was upset that he was not even aware how she had been doing, that he had not spent any time with her for over six weeks, and she wondered what kind of a husband he would make if they ever get married.

Mr. Pascal was a very patient man; he understood her complaints: sick with pregnancy and stuck with a man in a very complicated situation he couldn't even talk about with her. He consoled her and told her that he was committed to getting married and raising a family with her. He told her that he would support her with the pregnancy and look for a doctor to assist with the prenatal care. He advised her to stop working to make sure she would be free of stress and pressure. She was very happy to hear the kind words and encouragement. She had not been sure how he was going to receive this news. She forgot all about the hurt feelings she had towards him about being away for weeks. He promised that he would visit her after work the next day and spend more time with her.

The biggest obstacle for him at this point was how to break this to Mrs. Wilson. The pregnancy and engagement were not things he could hide. He thought he had to face reality for once. As he went back to Annapolis that evening, he was shaking with fear and confusion. He came home around 7:00 pm and told Mrs. Wilson that traffic on the Bay Bridge had been horrible and at a standstill. He had dinner, and after that, he told Mrs. Wilson that he was not feeling well that night. She asked him what was going on and if he could sit out on the deck with her to have some wine, and he obliged. There on the deck, as she sipped her wine, Mr. Pascal decided that he was going to bite the bullet and tell her what was going on with his life. He told her how he'd met his girlfriend in Washington, that her name was Gloria, and that she was pregnant with his child.

Shocked and dismayed, Mrs. Wilson dropped her half-full glass of wine on the deck. She told him to get the hell out of the house. That was it; Mrs. Wilson basically lost it. She kept screaming at him that he was lying son of a bitch, that she should not have trusted a black-ass, backward Haitian to begin with. She had forgotten the fact that she was the one who had forced him to move in, that if someone were lying, it was her lying to her husband of twenty years and cheating on him with his own chauffeur, that she was the one extorting a poor, undocumented immigrant and abusing him for his misfortunes. She had no idea that if she hadn't threatened him with deportation, he would not have succumbed to her advances. After a long night of verbal and sometimes physical abuse where she would pull him by the collar of his jacket, he decided to leave the house in the dead of night.

He went back to his friends in DC around 2:00 am. Everyone was awakened by his arrival, which was very unusual. They knew his story, but they did not expect him to be back at such an awful time. In the apartment, Mr. Pascal had two other roommates who were present that early morning. They came out to the living room, and one put on a fresh pot of coffee to figure out what was up with Pascal. He told them the whole story and that he was worried that Mrs. Wilson might actually follow through with her threat of reporting him to the INS. His friends told him that it wouldn't be easy for her to do that now that there was a child in the picture. None of these hopeful sentiments made Mr. Pascal feel any better. To him, the only good thing about his confession was that he was not going to be forced to live in that godforsaken home of the Wilsons.

The next morning, Mrs. Wilson called Mr. Pascal to tell him there were some chores she needed to be completed at the house and that since Mr. Wilson would be arriving in a week or so, she needed to tidy up the house and garden before his arrival. Mr. Pascal replied that he had to attend to Gloria's doctor's appointments for the next three days and asked for those days off. She told him that would be fine but that she knew great doctors Gloria could use for her care.

Mr. Pascal was not sure if she was trying to be apologetic in a way or up to some of the evil tactics she used to manipulate any situation. He told her that at this point, Gloria had already established a doctor for her pregnancy care, but if she needed it, they would be in touch. So, he got out of that one, luckily.

Mr. Pascal spent the rest of the week with Gloria, taking her to the doctor and caring for her. Gloria only knew the Wilsons through the employment that Mr. Pascal had with Mr. Wilson. She knew that he also did some home repairs for them and would sometimes stay over at their guest house when it was too late to drive from Annapolis back to Washington. She had no idea what her boyfriend, now fiancée, had been going through for close to a year they had been dating. She was busy with her own jobs and survival, trying to pay the bills and send money back home to her folks. There was no time to busy herself with what her boyfriend was doing and where he was staying.

As time went by, Mrs. Wilson got agitated with Pascal. Whenever she called him, he was distant and preoccupied. She never understood that the man had a child on the way and that, perhaps, it would be wiser to end the stupidity. However, he made the decision to put all his efforts into the care of Gloria and their unborn child. He would go with her for every prenatal care visit at Howard University Medical Center, where the only free prenatal care for young mothers without insurance existed. As the pregnancy continued to progress, the doctors provided prenatal vitamins and coached the expectant parents on how to get ready for their child. The gender was determined to be a boy, and both Gloria and Mr. Pascal were very happy.

On the seventh month of the pregnancy, Gloria started to experience swelling of her extremities and shortness of breath. The doctors initially thought that it was normal to have some swelling at that stage of the pregnancy; however, the condition grew worse. Her doctors preferred to refer her to a specialist who had more experience with risky pregnancies. As those specialists were highly sought after, the appointment they gave Gloria was over a month away. The other unfortunate fact of the American healthcare system was that if you lack good medical insurance, the specialty doctors didn't waste their time on you. It was very sad but the reality of America.

While Gloria was waiting to see the specialist, she got very sick. Mr. Pascal was working for Mr. Wilson that whole week, and the emergency call came to the Wilsons' house. Mr. Wilson, who was told about the situation, offered to help. Mr. Pascal was desperate at that moment and accepted the offer of having Mrs. Wilson get in touch with her former gynecologist and obstetrician. She jumped at the opportunity to help and arrange an emergency visit in Bethesda, where the doctor had an office.

Gloria was rushed to the clinic. Since Mr. Pascal and Gloria were not legally married, all her treatment consents were only to be signed by herself as long as she was in sound mind. The doctor insisted that she sign the consent forms inside the treatment room; he also requested that a female chaperone come with her. Mrs. Wilson jumped in and offered to accompany Gloria to the treatment room. The doctor and his assistants had Gloria sign all the documents for the new patient. Gloria had been educated up to high school in French, but knew enough English. However, she did not understand the forms she was signing and thought they had to do with her medical treatment.

As soon as the doctor examined her, he realized that Gloria had all the signs of preeclampsia. This is a condition where the pregnant mother has a high level of untreated hypertension. Without an emergency Cesarean section, both the mother and the baby could die immediately. The doctor ordered an ambulance right away; Mr. Pascal was confused but went along with the advice of the doctor. The ambulance took Gloria right to Washington Hospital Center; the doctor had already called the hospital about getting ready for the emergency, and since he had privileges there, he was the one to do the surgery.

By the time the ambulance pulled into the parking lot of the emergency room, the consent forms were ready for Mr. Pascal to sign. Since he was the father of the unborn child and since Gloria had no next of kin, he was the right person to sign them. All Mr. Pascal was worried about was how to save the mother and his child; he signed the forms, and Gloria was rolled into the operating room. It was apparent on the consent form that there were high risks associated with the procedure, leading to the possible loss of one of them, if not both.

Mr. Pascal and the Wilsons waited outside the operating room. After a long period of extremely tense waiting, the doctors came out to break the most awful news to Mr. Pascal: Gloria did not make it through the surgery. Her case of preeclampsia was end-stage, and they could not save her. They told him that the boy was doing well and all his signs were normal. The baby would just have to be in the neonatal unit for a bit longer.

Mr. Pascal broke down and was comforted by the Wilsons. All of a sudden, he had become both the father and mother of this baby boy. After the formalities of the deceased were finalized, it was the decision of Mr. Pascal to decide on a name for his firstborn son. He chose the famous Haitian name Toussaint Pascal. Since Toussaint had been born a month and a half premature from a high-risk pregnancy, his growth was compromised, and the neonatal physicians suggested that the baby spend at least three weeks at the neonatal care unit. Since Mr. Pascal had no idea where to take a newborn baby, and with the burial of Gloria looming over his head, he was relieved that the baby would be taken care of at the hospital in the interim.

Mr. Wilson told Mr. Pascal that he should not worry about any of the burial expenses. Gloria was given a great send-off, with all expenses paid for by Mr. Wilson. The Haitian community also helped Mr. Pascal with other expenses. Of course, nothing was going to bring Gloria back, but the help he got was much needed.

In the weeks after the funeral, Mr. Pascal went through a huge bout of depression. He'd lost the love of his life; his plan to spend the rest of his life with her had been shattered. He was despondent about life without her. He felt so much regret that he'd wasted so much time that he could have spent with her. He lamented promises unfulfilled and plans that had never materialized, dreams that had never been achieved. But every time he felt the bottom of it all, he would remember the face of his little boy, the innocence of it, the precious life that had been given by Almighty God at the same moment that another life had been taken away. There was a sense of religiosity about Mr. Pascal that he'd never realized before. He consoled himself with his inner faith that Almighty God would want him to live for the care of the living. From that moment, Mr. Pascal started to concentrate on how to plan a life for Toussaint and leave Gloria to rest in peace. He accepted the will of his creator.

As the baby was still in the prenatal care unit, Mr. Pascal occupied his time working for the Wilsons; he would visit the baby on a daily basis right after he dropped off Mr. Wilson. He would hold his son and feed him with the baby formula, and the nurses would leave them so Mr. Pascal could enjoy being with his son. On every weekend, the Wilsons would come with him to visit the baby. One Saturday, Mrs. Wison asked if she could hold the baby. Mr. Pascal said no problem; he told her that she could feed him with formula, too. As she held Toussaint, she cried with joy. She had tried for over ten years to have a baby of her own, until she had been told she could never have a child, so the emotions were extreme for her.

As time went by, the Wilsons had private discussions about what the next course of action would be for Mr. Pascal. The conversations between the couple centered on what would happen to the baby since Mr. Pascal had no family in America and was an illegal immigrant who could easily be deported. This discussion was always one-sided, with

Mrs. Wilson being the one coming up with probing questions. Mr. Wilson was genuinely eager to help Mr. Pascal without any nefarious intentions. However, Mrs. Wilson was up to something. This was told to Mr. Pascal by Ms. Yolanda, the Wilsons' Puerto Rican chef. Yolanda was not a live-in chef; she only came to cook for the Wilsons on special occasions. Yolanda and Mr. Pascal became good friends, and she felt for him without knowing the specific details of his predicament.

Mrs. Wilson would casually throw out the idea of adopting Toussaint, but her husband thought the whole thing preposterous, as the baby's father was alive and well.

Mrs. Wilson asked her husband to keep Mr. Pascal employed and to have both him and the baby move in. That way, Mr. Pascal would have time to figure out where to live on a permanent basis. Mr. Wilson was very kind and was fine with the idea. She told her husband to let Mr. Pascal know about the offer so as to not appear too pushy. Mr. Pascal was not sure about the idea, but he had no choice; his Washington apartment, which he shared with other guys, was not a place to have an infant, especially with the smoking and drinking that went on. But at the same time, he did not want to move back into the Wilsons' house. Mr. Wilson insisted that Mr. Pascal move in at least until he found a suitable place for the baby. Mr. Pascal could not continue to refuse, so he reluctantly agreed to move into the Wilsons' house again, this time officially.

The baby was brought home from the hospital, and Mr. Pascal and his son shared a ground suite in the house. While Mr. Pascal was working and chauffeuring Mr. Wison, Mrs. Wilson had a nanny for the baby, all paid by the Wilsons. As time went by, the baby grew tremendously, and Mrs. Wilson became extremely attached to Toussaint. Mr. Pascal was happy that his son was healthy and larger than other babies his age. He was grateful to the Wilsons and the nanny who took care of him.

After six months, Toussaint was turning on his own and smiling. It was a joyous milestone. Mr. Pascal got more and more experienced with being a single father, but as the baby grew older and started to walk, he felt that it was time for him and his son to find a new place to live. During that time, it was not easy to get an apartment without having proper immigration documents; in his previous apartment lived a friend who was a permanent resident and who sponsored the other, non-legal roommates. On top of that, Mr. Pascal had a history of being a foreign agent, as he had worked at the Haitian embassy; this would have raised red flags on his lease application, so it was either stay at the Wilsons with a growing toddler or go back with the single roommates. The Wilsons insisted that Mr. Pascal and his son could continue to live on the estate as long as they wanted, and Mr. Pascal once again reluctantly accepted the offer.

Mrs. Wilson took over a big part of Toussaint's growth by teaching him everything, from how to talk to how to walk, as his father was always away working with Mr. Wilson. She took a keen interest in the child's development. It was like a family within a family. Living with the Wilsons, which had once been a frustration for Mr. Pascal, became a relief once he realized the progress of his son's growth. He still felt restricted, living in someone else's house and not raising his son as he wished, but a poor man cannot be choosy.

Years went by, and by the young age of five, Toussaint was learning how to write, taught at home by Mrs. Wilson. At this juncture, the boy started calling Mrs. Wilson Mommy, and she was delighted to have been entrusted with that title; she loved every moment of it. With Mr. Pascal busy with Mr. Wilson's business, he could not be with his son as much. Toussaint, however, was extremely fond of his father.

Right after Toussaint turned six years old, in 1977, there was a huge debate in the US immigration system as to whether Haitian refugees were political or economic exiles. Most American administration officials at the time were of the opinion that most Haitians were fleeing poverty and not political persecution. The media was full of stories about how there were over three hundred thousand Haitians living in the United States, with half of those illegally, so the INS started a campaign to deport those who could be easily located through overstayed visas, such as Mr. Pascal. His was easy to pinpoint, as he was a registered foreign agent who had lost his diplomatic credentials.

One day, the phone rang at the Wilsons' house. It was one of Mr. Pascal's friends from Washington with whom he shared an apartment. The friend told Mr. Pascal that there were deportation papers for him and he was to cooperate without delay. Mr. Pascal almost dropped the phone when he heard the news. He rushed to Washington and wanted to see the papers for himself. It was a US government plan to deport as many illegal Haitian immigrants as they could.

Mr. Pascal had no attorney to argue for the case of his son and how little Toussaint could be losing his father after having already lost his mother. He shared the news with Mr. Wilson, who was ready and willing to hire an attorney for the case. It was not an easy case, as all of those who were initially placed on the deportation list had no case to make to stay. Obviously, Toussaint was an American citizen, as he had been born in America, even if by illegal immigrants. But as a minor, the little boy could not sponsor his father.

Mr. Pascal had a huge dilemma. The attorney hired by the Wilsons suggested that the only way he could assure a good future for his son was to let the Wilsons adopt him, leave for Haiti, and get his son to sponsor him after he became an adult. Now, whether the idea was Mrs. Wilson's or not was open for a debate. After a long period of frustration and fear at leaving his only son, Mr. Pascal reluctantly agreed to the adoption route and to leave his son with the Wilsons. It was the most difficult decision for him to make, as he was beginning to bond with his son and looking forward to enrolling him in elementary school. But fate had a different plan.

The custody papers were signed, and full adoption rights were afforded to the Wilsons. Mr. Pascal was deported back to Haiti, very bitter that he had to give up the custody of his only son.

Mr. Wilson wanted to help out Mr. Pascal and the little boy, who had no other relatives in America. Mrs. Wilson's intentions could not have been more different. She excitedly told all her friends of her soon-to-be motherhood, how she was planning to enroll Toussaint in one of the area's best private schools. One of the first things she did was legally change the boy's name from his biological father's patriotic name, Toussaint, to Elmer Wilson.

Dr. Estima's long history of Elmer's (formerly Tousaint's) real father and family made everything clear for Elmer. He finally realized that his real father had actually been forced to give up his only son. While Mr. Wilson's intentions had been purely humanitarian, Mrs. Wilson had had other plans all along. If her intentions were not evil, she would not be preventing Elmer from corresponding with his father. Besides, Mr. Pascal's understanding was that he would eventually reunite with his son in due time, that the Wilson's were doing him a favor. If anything, what Mr. Pascal was guilty of was naiveté. But having been misled by Mrs. Wilson notwithstanding, what other choices did Mr. Pascal have at that juncture?

Now that Elmer had the information he needed to locate his father in Haiti, he had a task on his hands. He thanked Dr. Estima for putting the puzzle together for him. All he had to do now was contact the right people in Haiti to assist in finding his father.

Luckily, Dr. Estima was still connected to his homeland, and he promised that he would be able to find someone who could connect Elmer to his lost father.

When Elmer returned to Baltimore, his closest friends, who were aware of the situation, were eagerly awaiting his return. They had hoped that the news would be good, that Elmer would finally have a lead on the whereabouts of his father. Elmer went straight to his friends' place. Interestingly, he'd kept his emotions in check while he'd been with Dr. Estima.

After digesting the whole story about how his mother died, how he was orphaned twice, and how difficult it must have been for his father to lose both his mother and his child and then having to retell the story to his friends, Elmer was extremely sad, to the point of tearing up. His friends were kind and attentive, understanding the emotional rollercoaster that Elmer was going through. They felt bad that his relationship with his adopted parents was based on lies and misrepresentations and might suddenly come to an end. As far as Elmer was concerned, he would not cut off relations with the Wilsons, but nothing was ever going to be the same.

As for his friends, their opinions differed based on many factors. Some of them told Elmer that he should be as close to normal as possible; after all, the Wilsons were extremely wealthy, and Elmer was the only legal heir of their estate. In purely economic terms, they wanted Elmer to hang in there and play the game. He could still continue his search to locate his father, but no confrontation was necessary with the Wilsons. Others suggested that Elmer should confront his adopted parents and expose the evil acts of Mrs. Wilson, who had destroyed the only true family Elmer was ever going to have, that he should show her that her selfish disregard for others had created unnecessary pain and she should feel the pain she had caused. They went further with their idea of revenge by going as far as Elmer suing the Wilsons for emotional and mental anguish for their decision to deny him a connection with his biological father.

Elmer was not interested in keeping silent and indifferent about his anguished life just because he wanted to inherit the Wilsons' wealth. He had a bright future, and inheritance was not at the top of his list in lieu of being truthful to himself. So, buying silence for inherited wealth from those who had violated him was not a priority. At the same time, he knew that he owed lots of his personal success to the Wilsons, especially the genuine intentions of Mr. Wilson. They had raised him, educated him, and led him to a life full of opportunities and with a bright future, so letting things cool down was worth considering. In the meantime, he could continue searching for his father in Haiti and moving forward as best he could.

To Elmer, the best way to avoid ruffling any feathers with his adopted family was to look for a job in an area geographically distant from them. Perhaps moving away from the East Coast would give him the buffer zone he needed from them. He thought about Chicago, where Grant Thornton had offered him a very attractive package, including stock shares and other incentives. He also liked the idea of being in the Midwest, where travel is easy within the country. The cold weather of Chicago was the only sticking point.

Another great offer came to Elmer from Ernst & Young. This firm was offering him the best package. With the majority of its activities being international, Elmer liked the idea of seeing the world and traveling. The recommendations of his advisors leaned more towards Ernst & Young. That was going to require Elmer to move to London, the firm's headquarters.

Elmer jumped at the opportunity and accepted the three-year contract to move to London. However, he stipulated that he would need to have four months to untie knots before he moved to the United Kingdom. Elmer wanted to spend that time following all the leads on his father, even if it meant going to Haiti. The company accepted Elmer's condition and offered to pay him during the four months before his starting date. It was a delightful offer.

Elmer started the search by visiting Dr. Estima again. Dr. Estima had been calling Haiti to locate someone who might know where Mr. Pascal lived. His influential connections had created great leads. Mr. Pascal was located in the city of Dessotce, which was twenty-eight kilometers away from the capital city of Port-au-Prince. Dr. Estima had also located Mr. Pascal's relatives in the capital, whom Elmer could speak to and start the process of reunification.

Elmer did not waste any time and started contacting those relatives. Mr. Pascal's remote city did not have great telecommunication systems; therefore, Elmer could only speak on the phone with one of the relatives. He told them that he was trying to locate Mr. Pascal. Since the Haitian community is a very family-oriented and closely knit community, the story of Elmer looking for his biological father had already reached Haiti, so when he contacted the relatives in Port-au-Prince, they were happy to receive the phone call. They told him that they would send for his father to come to the capital so that he could speak with him directly without anyone else being the intermediary.

Elmer was delighted to have help from his relatives, and although not all of them spoke English, the joyous feeling of finding their lost relative did not need any language translation. His aunts and cousins were all crying over the phone and could not wait for him to come to Haiti and meet with them. One thing that they avoided telling Elmer about his father was that he was suffering from stage four cancer. They did not want to devastate him that soon.

The next few days, Elmer started to plan a trip to Haiti. He did not tell anyone about the plan except his best friends, whom he had always conferred with about his most personal decisions. Again, his folks in Annapolis thought that since he was getting multiple job offers from different companies, he was busy with interviews and meetings. His friends were all extremely happy for him and threw a huge party at his apartment in Baltimore. They wished him all the success to finally meet his lost father. Elmer started thinking about what his father would look like. After all, he had only been six years old when he'd last seen him, and though there were some old photos he had seen many years ago, those photos were long gone, as his adopted mother had made a point of erasing memories of his father.

When Elmer had inquired about pictures of his biological parents, his adoptive mother had told him that due to a fire in the house, lots of family pictures had been destroyed, which was why there were no photos of his biological family. Here he was, about to enter the professional labor force at the age of twenty-three, and he couldn't even identify his father from the crowd. Elmer estimated that based on the information he'd gathered from Dr. Estima, his father would probably be in his late fifties to early sixties.

Elmer flew from Baltimore to Miami on a Thursday morning and arrived in Port-au-Prince for lunch. He was to be picked up by one of his relatives at the airport. When he walked into the lobby, there was a young man around the same age as Elmer with a sign that said, "Elmer Pascal, welcome to your second home," on it, flanked on both sides by two young ladies of the same age, each holding dozen of roses and balloons to welcome Elmer.

Elmer approached the young man, who introduced himself as Francisco Pascal, Elmer's first cousin. They embraced like family members meeting for the first time would. Francisco also introduced Maria, his fiancé, and her best friend, Vicky. Both girls were about the same age as Elmer and Francisco. Vicky was about to finish law school at the university. Beautiful and very charismatic, she kept Elmer's attention the whole time they were driving from the airport. They sat in the back of the car, while the engaged couple sat upfront. Elmer was impressed with Vicky's knowledge of Haitian history; it was like she was giving him an expert lesson on the Haitian struggle against the

French.

At the hotel, Elmer checked into his room and freshened up. The plan was to head to the family house in the suburbs of Port-au-Prince for a family gathering. Francisco told Elmer that everyone in the Pascal family who could come would be there and the whole weekend had been planned out for the family get-together. Francisco also assured Elmer that he and his father would be afforded some private time to catch up with each other. Elmer was very thankful for the opportunity to come to Haiti and be part of his true family. Coming to Haiti reminded him a little bit of his visit to West Africa. His emotions, however, were more tense and raw.

On their way to the compound, Elmer asked Francisco, whom he already considered a longtime friend, about Vicky. Francisco told him that he had the feeling that there had been chemistry going on in the back of the car on their way from the airport. Elmer blushed and kept asking about Vicky. Francisco told him that Vicky was his fiancé's best friend and she was attending law school. Vicky, he said, was a very intelligent girl and on her way to working in one of the biggest law firms in Haiti. Francisco added that in case Elmer was wondering, Vicky was single. Elmer replied that he was just curious, but Vicky was really pretty.

The car pulled up to the parking lot of a huge villa. Ladies with flowers and branches of fresh leaves in their hands said welcome in English and Creole. To Elmer's delight, Vicky was also there, and their eyes met in non-verbal communication. Elmer got out of the vehicle and said thank you with his hands together.

As they moved to the backyard of the compound, he saw a middle-aged man with a cane sitting under a palm tree. The man was wearing a light brown suit and matching shoes. Tall, about six feet, he seemed to have lost the weight that had once complemented his height. Gradually he got up, and his eyes caught Elmer's. The gentleman walked over to Elmer with an unsteady gait. At that moment, Elmer and his father knew who the other was. The father exclaimed in English, "Oh, son, how great to see you." As the two embraced, they started to weep. Then the entire family started to weep with joy at the reunification and celebration.

A priest had been invited by the family to mark the occasion with some prayers. He said, "God is great, the one who made this father and his lost son meet each other. We should be grateful that we are witnessing this happy moment. May they continue to cherish a life of happiness and love together for a long, long time."

The program started with a huge feast, and Elmer was introduced to many aunts, uncles, cousins, and relatives on both sides of his family. As part of the arrangements, Elmer's relatives on his late mother's side had also been invited to come, and he had the opportunity to meet them. There were so many emotions in the air: happiness and joy at the family reunion but also sadness for the time lost. As the priest had indicated to the participants in the gathering, everything had happened for a reason.

After the feast, the family arranged a nice and festive Haitian dance with Elmer and his father in the center of the circle and everyone singing and clapping hands. Elmer, of course, didn't understand Creole, but he went along and danced to the Afro-infused beat, which sounded like the music he had experienced during his visits to West Africa.

At that moment, when everyone was at their happiest and dancing to the music, Francisco, who was dancing with his fiancé and her best friend, Vicky, stole Elmer and placed his hand on Vicky's, a traditional local way to introduce a prospective couple on a dance floor. Elmer was happily surprised and danced with Vicky; they had a great time singing and dancing, with the DJ changing the music to American beats.

After the festive Haitian and American dance and music, it was time for the group to give Elmer and his father the privacy to be with each other. They decided to take a walk on the beach and just catch up. Elmer knew from the moment he saw his father sitting down with a cane in his hand that he was not feeling well, as it was uncommon for a man his father's age to need a cane for stability. He also noticed that his father was too thin for his height, so he asked his father if he was alright.

Mr. Pascal suspected that all the letters he'd sent his son in America might not have been received, but there was no way of knowing it. All he knew was that he'd sent his son numerous letters in the mail telling him that he was sick with cancer and did not wish to die before he spoke directly with his son. From the way Elmer asked his question, Mr. Pascal knew that his son had no knowledge of the situation, so he told him that he had been sending birthday cards and letters on every occasion, that he'd even sent Elmer registered letters explaining that he was sick with cancer and might not live long.

Elmer knew that his mother had hidden the letters from him, and he was shocked that she was so callous that she would hide the information that his father might be dying and might not be able to say a final goodbye. She'd even hid the health issues from Mr. Wilson, for she knew that Mr. Wilson would not allow her to do such an evil thing.

So, Mr. Pascal told his son that he had been diagnosed with stage four lung cancer and the best gift he could hope to have was to see his only son before it was time. Elmer broke down in tears. He felt so bad that he'd had no idea how his father had been suffering all alone.

Mr. Pascal told his son that it was not his fault that he had not received the correspondence. It was meant to be that they would reunite and rejoice with whatever time God had allotted them to spend with each other. Mr. Pascal told his son that the pain was much worse for him, knowing that he had to leave his son behind, but if there was any solace in the separation, Toussaint, as he called Elmer, had received a good education and opportunity in the US. Who would have known what might have become of him had he left with his biological father.

Elmer, though, felt cheated of his true identity by the Wilsons. The material things meant nothing to him, nor did the fake love of his adopted mother, who had only adopted him to fill in the gaping hole of childlessness, not to nurture him. Elmer felt that if she'd had an iota of love, consideration, and care for him, she would not have nearly destroyed the connection between him and his real father.

Elmer shared with his father all the memories, feelings, and emotions he had gone through as a young boy who, after a while, started to realize that he was missing something. Although the Wilsons provided everything material, they could not fill the void. Elmer explained to his father how difficult it was for him to understand why his father had left and why he would not come back to at least explain the circumstances surrounding his departure, why his biological mother had died and how. None of that was clearly explained to him by his adoptive parents. It seemed as though, if it were not for the color of his skin, they would have forced him to believe that they were his biological parents.

After a long night of catching up, getting it all out, and clearing up all the misconceptions, they were both happy with the final turn of events. Elmer decided that he would stay for a couple of weeks and spend quality time with his father. They hiked in the mountains of Port-au-Prince, and they went to the beach. It was the happiest Elmer had been in a long time.

One morning, at a bed and breakfast on the beach, Elmer asked his father if he ever had another family after the death of his mother in America. His father told him that after he lost Elmer's mother, he never envisioned himself with another woman. Right after he was deported, he came back home and started teaching at a local high school. After he was diagnosed with cancer, he was let go on a disability. Elmer wanted to tell his father that considering how nice his biological mother was said to have been, she would not have minded if his father had started a new life again with someone; she would not have been that selfish. But under the circumstances, and considering the condition his father was in, it was not going to change much. This feeling was Elmer's way of longing for a blood-related sibling, someone he could cling to as a family if his father passed on before him.

Elmer told his dad that he would look into finding different doctors to see if there could be any cure for his cancer. The father was not keen about the idea, as he had been told he did not have much time left. Elmer still wanted a second opinion, so he took his father to one of the top oncologists in Haiti. After multiple tests and exams, the doctors at that clinic gave them some hope, saying that one of the lungs was still operable and the other could be removed via transplant if there was a donor. If Mr. Pascal could be placed on the waiting list, a donor might come along.

The only sticking point that the doctors were not sure about was how the treatment was going to be paid for; it wouldn't be cheap. Elmer asked them what the procedure would cost, and the doctor told him it was between twenty to twenty-seven thousand dollars.

However, deep in his heart, Mr. Pascal was not sure if he would last that long. As the Somali proverb says, "A wise man knows his fate for death." Nevertheless, Elmer told the doctors that he would be willing to pay for his father's transplant surgery if they could put him on the list. For Haitian doctors, this was a great opportunity because most Haitians can't afford such an expensive procedure. So, having an American pay for the surgery in dollars was a great financial incentive. Mr.Pascal was otherwise healthy, with no other underlying systemic diseases; therefore, there was no contraindication to treating him.

As soon as arrangements were made for Mr. Pascal to be on the list, Elmer started planning for his trip back to America to start his new job; however, he wanted to spend more time with Vicky, with whom he had been communicating during his time in Haiti. He told Francisco to arrange a dinner date for the four of them. Francisco made the arrangements and reserved one of the best restaurants in Port au Prince. The ladies were to arrive together and meet Elmer and Francisco for the event.

They had dinner together and danced to the music of the restaurant's live band. After dessert was served, the engaged couple told the new couple that they had another appointment to make and left Elmer and Vicky to carry on. Elmer and Vicky continued talking until the late hours of the night and really hit it off. He asked her what type of law she was going to specialize in, and she replied that she was interested in international corporate law. She wanted to travel the world, and that specialization would allow her to do so.

Elmer told her that because of his connections with international accounting firms, he might be able to help her with networking and introduce her to different companies. He told her that he was actually heading to his new post in London with an accounting firm. She told him that she had looked up that very company not long ago. It appeared the two had connected both personally and professionally. They set up to meet for a few more dates before Elmer's departure back to the States, and they promised to stay in touch.

Elmer told his father that he would visit every holiday and, as soon as a donor was found, he would be flying back for the surgery. It was delightful news for everyone that there was hope for Mr. Pascal after all he had been through in his life.

Elmer came back to Baltimore to get ready for his relocation to London. He still had two months left. Ordinarily, he would have taken a cruise or a Hawaiian vacation to fill that gap and enjoy himself before the busy life awaiting him in the UK, but because of the situation with his father in Haiti and the fact that, at any moment, they might call him about a possible donor, he wanted to stand by and be ready for any eventuality. His adoptive parents, oblivious to what was happening, kept asking him to join them for a river cruise in Northern Europe, but Elmer always had an excuse, so they gave up.

They told him that they had a gift for him for his graduation and for passing his CPA exam. Elmer could not refuse that, and knowing his adoptive father, it was probably going to be in the form of a check, so he drove to Annapolis to see them. As usual, they had an elaborate dinner party on the waterfront with all their friends. The guest of honor, of course, was Elmer, and the occasion was his graduation party. There were caterers of every kind, and after everyone ate like a horse, the Wilsons called Elmer over and gave him a key to a brand-new BMW and an envelope that was only to be opened by him in private.

Elmer was polite; of course, he was not going to refuse such nice gifts, but he also did not want to arouse any suspicion about his father's situation, so he acted like a grateful son enjoying the party. At the end, he thanked his parents for all they had done for him, he thanked the guests for spending their evening with him, and he informed everyone that he had accepted a position with Ernst & Young's global headquarters in London and would be leaving in a couple of months. Everyone cheered and congratulated him. Elmer said goodbye to everyone and, once again, thanked his parents.

When he returned to his apartment late that night, he opened the envelope that had been handed to him by Mr. Wilson. He knew it was going to be a check, but he could not foresee the amount. Remember, he was waiting for doctors in Haiti to find a donor for his father's lung transplant, and the cost of the surgery was not going to be cheap. Not to mention he had not yet started working. So, if the doctors called, he would not know what to do for payment. Therefore, the amount of money on that check was going to be very instrumental in covering the expense for the surgery.

Elmer prayed so hard that the amount would at least cover the cost. As he unfolded the white paper inside the envelope holding the check, he trembled, and his hands got sweaty. He unfolded the long business check with Mr. Wilson's company logo on top of it. The check was in the amount of fifty thousand dollars. He was ecstatic and, he screamed, "Thank you, God!" at the top of his lungs. He was so happy that he was going to be able to help his father and potentially save his life.

The months before his departure for London, Elmer and Vicki communicated non-stop. The two developed a very loving relationship. Elmer felt that there was a big reason for all that he had gone through; of course, he knew that everything happens for a reason, but it occurred to him that up until it happens to you, the realization that it is fate is hard to accept. All the tests and tribulations he'd lived through had taken him to Haiti, a place he'd never imagined he was ever going to visit, culminating in him finding love, not only with his long-lost father, but also with Vicky, a potential lifelong partner.

He and Vicky spoke on the phone for long hours, even when it was not cheap to call long distance. They felt they had found their soulmates. They spoke about marriage, family, children, and everything couples usually talk about. He told her of his life with the Wilsons, how he was never told the truth about his identity, how he longed to have the scent of his true, biological mother. He shared how regretful he sometimes felt growing up about living a life that, while privileged, still lacked a genuine feeling of contentment, how his life growing up was based on lies. He felt that living in Haiti among his own people in poverty would have been a much happier life than what he had gone through.

Vicky was very easy to talk to, and she listened to him with complete attention. She calmed him down by pointing out that none of those life experiences were under his control and that those tough times had only made him much stronger. They had opened his eyes to explore his true identity, and while the journey might have been a very rough road, it was the destination that mattered more. Finding his true identity was worth more than anything else in the world. Her calming words and philosophical perspective made Elmer realize that Vicky was going to be the one he wanted to take along with him through the next journey of his life.

The time went by very quickly, and Elmer ended up moving to London for his job. He found a place in Central London, where most international financial firms have offices. He met a lot of young African Brits, who, like Elmer, were very Afrocentric. Some of them were second-generation Brits with parents from Nigeria, Ghana, and The Gambia. He also fell in love with London, a cosmopolitan city with a very desirable culture and cuisine. He was introduced not only to various African and Caribbean cuisines, but also to the Southeast Asian curries from India, Pakistan, and Bangladesh. His friends in London always teased that the amount of spicy curry he was consuming was never close to what they would have expected from an American from Baltimore. He always got back at them by saying that his palate might have been trained in the East Coast of America, but his real genes were Haitian.

After only two months with Ernst & Young in London, Elmer received a phone call from Haiti informing him that his father had passed. He immediately took a leave of absence to go to the funeral. It was a very sad moment; however, as Elmer would recall later, he was lucky to have had the chance to see his father before it was too late. Elmer was at peace with what had happened. He knew in his heart that he wanted to help his father, but he could not have delayed the process of death.

After the funeral, Elmer stayed another week to settle his father's estate. He also spent time with Vicky and talked with her about what level to take their relationship. Vicky was a very traditional Haitian who came from a well-known family in the capital city. Elmer respected her and told her that he intended to continue communication with her but his ultimate goal was for them to spend their lives together. This announcement put Vicky at ease; she realized that Elmer wanted a life with her, and she was happy that he did not beat around the bush. She told him that she appreciated his frankness and she would be waiting to hear from him.

Elmer flew back to London with mixed feelings. He had lost his father, which, in reality, was not a huge surprise, but he'd also come out of Haiti with a sense of accomplishment. Meeting Vicky was one of the best things that he could recall ever happening to him. He'd had girlfriends and relationships before. After all, he had been raised by a rich white family who had afforded him all kinds of things that girls wanted: cars, vacations, and money. To Elmer, however, truth and genuine, non-superficial feelings meant more. He saw those qualities in Vicky. He saw in her a true friend he could confide in and share his innermost feelings and contemplations with. He saw in Vicky a future wife – the mother of his future children, God willing.

Elmer started to plan how he could bring Vicky to America as his wife. Their long-distance correspondence continued, and he traveled to Haiti several times during his assignment with Ernst & Young in London. The plan was for him to get engaged in Haiti and process immigration papers for Vicky in the American embassy there.

Elmer did very well in London, and during his couple of years there, he was promoted to account executive for the New York office. He was transferred to the biggest financial city in the world, and Vicky was approved for permanent residency, too. By then, she was a qualified attorney, but she had to pass the New York Bar Exam to practice in America. The couple settled in Manhattan and started a family there. Vicky was able to get her license to practice law both in New York and Maryland, where she had relatives.

After a couple of years in New York and with twin boys, the couple decided that they wanted to be closer to family. Vicky's uncle and cousins lived there, as did Elmer's adoptive parents, with whom he remained in touch, though it was a distant relationship. As expected, his adoptive mother did not approve of Elmer marrying a Haitian. Elmer joked about Mrs. Wilson's early-onset dementia, as she might have forgotten that her adoptive son was Haitian himself. Vicky thought that was cruel on Elmer's part, to which Elmer usually replied that he had learned cruelty from his adoptive mother.

The other reason they wanted to move to Maryland was that New York City was no longer a place to raise a young family. They wanted a house with a large backyard where the boys could play and swim. The congested city was not appealing to them. Elmer also wanted to have his own accounting firm, and Maryland, with its proximity to the federal government and large contractors, offered a great opportunity. So, they settled in the Silver Spring area of Montgomery County, with great schools and diverse communities.

Elmer was very successful with his accounting firm, and very soon, his business grew to other counties and cities in the state. Vicky also entered the workforce, as an attorney, after the boys started high school. She was employed by the IMF as one of the organization's general counsels. With her fluent English and French, she was highly sought after by other organizations, but she accepted a position with the International Monetary Fund in downtown Washington.

Everything was going well for the family. They took vacations to Haiti to introduce the boys to the Haitian culture and meet with their relatives there. The boys were very good in school, and both were getting very high marks. They both were accepted by elite colleges in the area. Both Vicky and Elmer instilled in their boys the desire to excel and the value of education. While they did well in school, the boys were also the product of their community and had friends and schoolmates who shaped their personalities. Elmer was keenly aware of the danger young black boys face in America, especially since the murder of Michael Brown in Ferguson. He always told the boys to be careful and avoid conflict with the police, but as is common among young people, the boys were not as worried or concerned as their parents were.

One of the boys, Jimmy, was more gregarious than his twin brother, Jeff. Jimmy had all sorts of friends in the area. One Halloween evening, the family received a phone call from the Baltimore Police Department that Jimmy was in jail. He had been involved in an argument with police and had resisted arrest. Elmer drove to the police station and inquired about the situation. Jimmy had been in Baltimore to visit his former classmate who was celebrating a birthday at the university there, and on his way back home to Silver Spring, he was stopped by a police officer, who questioned why he had been changing lanes so erratically. Jimmy said that he told the police he was not aware that this was the case but he was sorry if he had done that. The police officer argued with him, and after back-and-forth statements, he arrested the young man, accusing him of being belligerent and disrespectful of authority.

Elmer and Vicky wanted to bring a complaint against the police officer, but they were dissuaded by their family attorney to drop the case because the police will not be held accountable for any wrongdoing and, in the end, it was going to be a waste of time. This unjust abuse unnerved Vicky, who was new to the whole idea of American police brutality. Of course, she had been following the news stories about young black men being mistreated and, at times, killed at the hands of the police, but this was too close to home.

At that point, both Vicky and Elmer started to feel uneasy about raising teenage boys in America. The couple started looking into support groups in the community as well as online sources for help.

# 3

# RICHARD

*"In the end, we will remember not the words of our enemies, but the silence of our friends."* **Dr. Martin Luther King, Jr.**

As they sip their coffee, Richard and Khalid look at Elmer with disbelief and curiosity. Then they look at each other. Richard asks, "Where do you want to start, Elmer? That America has the highest number of COVID-19 deaths in the entire world? Or that George Floyd's killer is still enjoying freedom at home with his family? Or that we just had the highest unemployment rate and most people applying for unemployment since the Great Depression? Wait, you probably know the last point, as you are an accountant."

Elmer replies, "Wait, what happened? You mean they haven't arrested that killer? I can't believe this. Man, I have been busy catching up with my clients' tax returns. You know they extended the filing this year due to COVID, and everyone and their grandma is wanting to file all at the same time. I have not been watching any news for weeks. Heck, for over a month now."

Richard interjects, describing how things have gotten out of control with Donald Trump's rhetoric. If things were once bad for African Americans, they have only gotten worse. He also points out how, at the least, just existing in this land creates stress for blacks. "Really, after how many centuries, when can we finally rest in peace?"

He describes how, one night, he was heading home after showing houses to a prospective buyer and was pulled over by two police officers. "As I pulled to the side of the road, I placed my hands on both sides of the steering wheel to make sure that they didn't think I was a danger to them. They told me to roll down the window. After I did, one of them said to also roll down the back windows. So, I did as I was told. While one of the police officers asked me why I was swerving on the road, the other had his flashlight on, looking through the back seats of the car. I told him that there was nobody back there. He replied, 'I didn't ask you a question.' He kept putting his head inside the back window as though he wanted to smell something; you know, when someone is sniffing to catch some kind of scent.

"It was apparent to me that the reason they stopped me was to try and find something they could use against me. A beer bottle that was open, a piece of a joint they could create a case with. This is an everyday occurrence; it is routine harassment. I tell my sons and nephews to always stay calm when they get pulled over. Always comply with the police and show that you are not breaking any law. You have the right to exist, but don't pick a fight with the police; they have the guns, and they don't hesitate to use them, not even to injure, but to kill."

Richard turns his attention back to Elmer. "But how long could you play dummy? How long could you continue to face the abuse of those paid to protect you? How long could you endure injustice?"

Richard, an Air Force veteran of twenty years, says, "I even place a US Air Force veteran sticker on each of our family vehicles to be seen by the police when they pull us over for driving while black, to at the least show them that we are a family that has worn the uniform of this nation to protect and defend the Constitution of the United States against enemies both foreign and domestic. But even the uniform doesn't help you as long as you are black in America."

Richard was a former Air Force sergeant who retired after a long career as a helicopter technician. After retirement, he settled in Fort Washington, Maryland, and started a real estate business. He is well known in his community and is a regular youth mentor, especially for college-bound black boys. He says he owes his success in life to those who mentored him as a young man. He describes how racial profiling and mistreatment by the police have left him with a sense of displeasure about life in America, to say the least.

As a young boy raised by a single mom in the South, he had no male role model to look up to. He never knew his biological father, a biracial truck driver Richard's mom had briefly dated. His mother did the best she could to keep him out of trouble by moving out of the government housing projects in downtown Memphis, Tennessee. He says she held multiple jobs just to make ends meet so that he and his younger brother from a different father could get a good education and stay out of trouble.

Richard was never a troublemaker, but as he puts it, "As a young black man in America, trouble sometimes finds you even when you are not in search of it."

Richard recounts one late evening when he and his mother were walking back from a house where his mom used to be a domestic worker for a white family in the suburbs of Memphis. She cleaned the house for the family once a week to get extra cash. On this particular evening, Richard was helping his mom clean the three-story house as the family was away on vacation. They loved Richard's mom, as she was great in the way she took care of the house, including watering the yard and keeping everything to their satisfaction. Since Richard was off from school that week, he was able to help his mother.

When it was time for them to go home, they turned all the lights off and headed to the car outside. Just as Richard was coming out of the house, two police cars pulled into the driveway. One officer yelled, "Put up your hands, boy! Put up your hands!"

Richard was seventeen years old at the time, but with a six-foot-five, muscular physique, he looked like a twenty-five-year-old boxer or football player. He did as they said; Reverend Higonbothom had lectured him so many times about how to deal with the brutal behavior of the police: to stay calm and respectful and do as they say to avoid aggravating them. Reverend Higonbothom always made the point that it would be futile to argue that the police were wrong after you were shot and killed by those officers.

The police officers had Richard walk away from the house with his hands on his head. His mother was still inside the house, arranging mail for the owners of the house and turning the lights off. As she came out to lock the door, she saw the police cars and her son handcuffed on the side of the road. She exclaimed, "What are you doing to my son? Why is he handcuffed? What is happening?"

The second officer told Richard's mom, "Put up your hands, lady, and walk away from the house." She complied but was confused about what was happening.

The officers told Richard and his mother that the police station had received a phone call from the neighbors that there was a robbery underway at this address and that they were only responding to the call.

Richard's mother told the officers that they were not robbing the house, that she was the housekeeper and cleaner for the family and had been there before, as the family had given her the key to the house. She explained that the family was currently on vacation in the Bahamas and she was getting the house clean and ready for their return. She inquired as to who had called the police and accused them of robbing the house that she has been entrusted to take care of. She told them that her son was there to help her clean the house while off from school.

The police officers declined to say who had called them and insisted that they needed to take both Richard and his mother to the police station to make a report. They proceeded to place Richard in the back of the police car. Richard was confused and scared at the same time; he asked his mother why the officers were doing this to them. He said that they were not criminals, that they were earning a legitimate wage with the permission of the homeowner, that if the police wanted to make sure that they were not robbers, the family could be called to prove that there was no break-in. The police officers insisted that any calls and reports would have to be made at the station.

So, the police officers took Richard and his mom, both handcuffed and in the back of the police car, to the crowded station, where the real criminals were, and they were held there for hours. Richard and his mom were hungry and thirsty, but they were not allowed to have anything to eat. They felt like animals in a cage; the conditions were dehumanizing.

Finally, the station leader came and told them that if they could prove that they were at the house legitimately, they would be released. To do that, they had to make phone calls to the owners of the house, who were vacationing in the Bahamas. Unfortunately, the family did not answer the call. The police officer in charge of the case told Richard's mom that it was up to the chief to decide whether to release them.

Richard's mom demanded to speak with the police chief. After waiting for many more hours, finally, he came. He told them, "Look, you know you had no business being in that house, or in that neighborhood, for that matter. I can't release you until you provide concrete proof you had permission to be there."

Richard's mom demanded to speak to her lawyer. The chief asked her if she actually had one; perhaps he presumed that a poor black woman would not be able to afford a lawyer. She answered that she did, and she demanded her right to call her lawyer. The phone was provided, and she called the reverend. It was half past midnight, and the only times the reverend received a call that late was when there was a death among the congregants. As any responsible community leader would do, the reverend answered with fear. "Is everything ok, dear?" he asked.

"No. We have been arrested and criminalized for no reason." Richard's mom told the reverend what had happened, and he said he would be there as soon as he could. The reverend called the church attorney and informed him that he would need to accompany him to the local police station.

The Reverend got to the station before the attorney. He informed the police chief that the attorney was on his way, and then he asked why his congregants had been arrested. The police chief recognized the reverend from a previous case, and they chatted for a bit. He asked the reverend if he was close to the family in question, and the reverend replied that he was. The chief felt extremely bad about the whole thing, as this was an obvious case of racial profiling.

You see, the neighbors knew that Richard's mom had always cleaned that house and her son came on occasion to help her out, so they would not have been the ones calling the police. The chief was willing to release the family; the reverend, however, was looking beyond that and wanted to know what the hardworking single mother and her teenage boy had done to deserve being harassed and jailed while trying to earn a living wage.

As the family was getting ready to be released from the police station, the attorney arrived. Before Richard's mother could sign the release absolving the police officers of any wrongdoing, the attorney stopped her and told her not to sign anything before he could look through the document. From experience, the attorney had seen many situations where police officers had violated the civil rights of citizens and then had them sign documents that usually cleared the police of such violations.

The police officers should have had a record of the alleged break-in: who called and when they called. Even if the name of the caller were protected for privacy reasons, the address and time of the call would be recorded by the dispatcher. The attorney wanted to determine if the police had just been racially profiling the mother and her son. The police chief could not produce the evidence to convince the attorney that an actual person had indeed called and reported any break-in. Had Richard's mom signed the release document, it would have canceled any police accountability for the illegal and unjust mistreatment and jailing of the young man and his mother.

The chief suggested that the tired family go home; they would continue with the case in the morning. The attorney accepted the idea but insisted that a civil rights complaint be lodged against the two police officers who had forcibly arrested an innocent family.

Furthermore, the attorney took photos documenting the multiple handcuff injuries sustained by Richard on both arms while being arrested. The attorney informed the chief that he would be contacting the local ACLU (American Civil Liberty Union) office to inform them of this new case of police abuse.

The family was released, still in shock that they'd had to go through such an unpleasant experience. On their way home, Richard and his mother had a long discussion on the way African Americans are treated by the police. To protect her young son's mind, although she was well aware of the problem facing black people in America, especially young black men, she wanted to portray a rosy picture for him, that things would get better by the time he was ready to start a family. She insisted that if Richard concentrated on education, got a good job, and realized the American dream, none of this police nonsense would happen to him. He would overcome racial profiling and the systemic racism that uneducated and poor blacks face.

Richard disagreed vehemently. He pointed out to his mother that even if he got a PhD or became a brain surgeon or the richest man in America, he would still be black. Richard said, "The first thing they see is not who you are, what education level you have attained, or what Ivy League college you have attended. They see what color your skin is." His mother's long, awkward silence proved that he was exactly right.

They arrived home that night extremely exhausted; however, Richard could not fall asleep. Many thoughts raced through his mind. Why is life never fair? Would this have happened to him if he'd had a father who supported the family? Would his mother have to work so hard and at so many places during odd hours? It was too much for a seventeen-year-old to digest.

The next day, the attorney called them up and told them to come and meet at his downtown Memphis office. He wanted to discuss what had happened and how the police had profiled them. Reverend

Higonbothom told Richard to dress nicely, as they were meeting a professional attorney and it is always good to present oneself in the best light. He told the young man to put on nice trousers, a long-sleeved white shirt, and a formal necktie. Richard obliged and dressed up for the occasion.

At the meeting, the attorney asked them many questions while taking notes. Richard's mother described how she had an informal employment arrangement with the white family to clean the house weekly and look after the garden and mailbox while the family was away. She reported that she knew most of the neighbors, as they had known her to come and help the family, and there would be no reason for any of them to call the police on her and her son.

Richard recounted that when his mother turned right on the main road leading to the neighborhood, a police car followed them all the way to the corner stop sign at the entrance to the community and then to the house. It appeared as though the police wanted to make sure that the driver was the right one as he kept turning his headlights on.

It so happened that the house was the second on the street and Richard and his mother pulled into the driveway before the police could pull them over, so the officers decided to wait until they finished whatever they were doing. City police had been pulling over black drivers to write tickets and collect funds from the black residents to finance the police department budget. This was very common in Ferguson, Missouri, where, after the death of Michael Brown, a full investigation uncovered a scheme by the city police to basically collect ransom money from the black residents by writing unnecessary traffic violation tickets. For those poor and financially strapped residents, it was a must that they pay for those tickets to be able to drive and keep their jobs to again pay for those unjust tickets.

Being fully aware of the unfair and discriminatory acts of some police officers, the attorney started an inquiry into police mistreatment of Richard and his mother. After long back-and-forth discussions between the police and the church attorney, full interviews with the neighbors on both sides of the street where the alleged break-in occurred, and the owners of the house attesting that there was no break-in and that Richard and his mother had the keys to the house and were given permission to enter and clean the house, the police chief admitted that this was a case of bad judgment on the part of the police and the intention was to assure the security of the neighborhood.

It became apparent that this was a case of racial profiling. The attorney discovered that there had been no call to the station, as the dispatcher could not produce evidence of one. Purely and simply, this was a violation of civil rights, the right to be innocent until proven guilty. It proved that had Richard and his mother been white, the police would not have decided that they were breaking into the house. Not only had the police violated their rights, but they had inflicted physical injury as well as emotional and mental anguish. The attorney proceeded to log a civil case against the police department on behalf of Richard and his mom. Knowing that they had no leg to stand, the police officers involved settled the case for an undisclosed amount.

This was not the end of Richard's discriminatory encounters with police while he was still a young man at home. One evening, he was driving his mother to work as he'd just gotten his license and she wanted him to have some confidence in the rules of the road. Both his mother and Reverend Higonbothom had lectured him on how to deal with police while driving as a young black man. They instilled in him to always be respectful of the police, keep his hands visible and follow driving rules.

After he dropped his mom off at her job, he went over to his girlfriend's house to watch a movie and wait while his mother finished her work. After the movie, at around 9:00 pm, he left to pick up his mom. As he exited his friend's neighborhood, he realized a police car was flashing its lights behind him. Richard became extremely nervous. After the previous bad experience, he was freaking out and was like, *What now?* He managed to pull over slowly, without hitting a pole or a tree in the process.

The policeman had his headlights on as well as a flashlight as he slowly approached Richard's car. He ordered, "Roll down your windows, son." Richard did as requested while holding both hands on the wheel, just as Reverend Higinbotham had told him. The officer asked, "Where are you heading, son?" Richard said he was on his way to pick up his mother from work. "Let me see your license and registration," the policeman said. Richard asked if he could reach into his pocket to get his wallet to produce, and the policeman replied that he could. Richard was careful not to put his life in danger or give the officer an excuse to shoot him as he looked for his wallet inside his pocket. He also informed the officer that the car belonged to his mom and assumed the registration form would be inside the glove compartment. Before reaching for the compartment, he told the officer what he was going to do.

After Richard showed the officer both items, the police told him that as he was leaving the neighborhood, he did not make a full stop. Richard would have to pay a fifty-dollar ticket, and points would be marked on his record. Richard did not remember a stop sign at which he had failed to make a full stop; however, he was not going to argue with a policeman. The officer instructed Richard to either pay the ticket fully on time or show up for court on the date shown on the ticket.

Richard took the ticket and slowly pulled away from the curb. He picked up his mom from work and kindly asked her if she could drive the car home. For a teenage boy who'd just started driving, passing up a chance to drive a vehicle was unusual. His mother asked him if he was sure that he wanted her to drive. Richard responded that he was tired. With a mother's instinct, she knew something was the matter, but rather than going straight to the heart of it, she went around and asked him how the movie was. Richard was awfully quiet as they headed home. He could not hide the sadness he was feeling, but he didn't want his mother to worry and feel sad as well, so he made up a story about how the movie never happened as he'd had a big fight with his girlfriend.

His mother finally understood why he was down. She tried to calm him and tell him that life is all about the little hiccups but, sooner or later, things get smoothed over. She advised him and his girl to work it out.

Richard did not want his mother to go through another episode of police maltreatment, but he had to come to terms with how to pay for the ticket, so he told the reverend about the incident. The reverend completely understood how considerate Richard was in protecting his mother from the undue stress. The reverend offered to write the check to the police department, which would eliminate the need for Richard to present himself in court. Richard wanted to eventually share the incident with his mom, but due to the fact that they were both still suffering from the trauma of the previous encounter with the police, he decided to wait a bit.

As it got closer for Richard to graduate from high school, his mother and the church community had high hopes that he would start choosing which college to apply to. Obviously, because of financial constraints, Richard could not go out of state for college, so state colleges or community colleges were the only two financially viable options. His mother, however, had a plan. After he completed high school, she wanted him to go to Fisk University in Nashville, a historically black college. His mother even discussed the idea with church leadership, and everyone agreed that they were more than willing to pitch in and help Richard attend Fisk.

However, unbeknownst to his mother and everyone else, Richard had been communicating with an Air Force recruiter who'd come to the school on career day. It is very common for all the branches of the US military to go to minority high schools and convince juniors and seniors to enlist in the military. Since many of the affluent white schools are more inclined to send their kids to college and not the military, the recruiters, who get paid according to how many kids they get to enlist, go to poor and underprivileged high schools.

Those recruiters present a rosy picture of life in the military; some even promise untrue sign-on bonuses, claim that the government will pay for college, and extoll the opportunity to "travel the world." That latter promise, "traveling the world," is well known among Navy recruiters. They also lie about the fact that everyone who enlists gets to choose what trade or training they want to pursue. For example, if a kid wants to sign up as medical tech in the Navy, they don't tell them the truth about how the "needs of the Navy" trump one's choice of trade.

Another reason military recruiters prefer to go to underserved schools is that some of those kids, unfortunately, are from broken homes. They are seeking a sense of belonging, so the recruiters are trained to aim at those soft spots. They take advantage of the feelings of those poor boys and girls.

So, Richard secretly signed with an Air Force recruiter without the knowledge of his mother. As the college application season started, his mom was curious about why he hadn't started the process. She wanted to know how many teachers he would be getting letters of recommendation from and if he wanted her to speak to the pastor of their church about the letter to Fisk he'd promised to write.

Richard had been going along with the idea for the longest time, but once she mentioned the pastor and the letter, he froze. He looked up to the pastor, the Reverend Dr. David Higonbothom, as not only a religious figure and community leader, but also a father figure. He confided in the pastor and shared all his teenage troubles. And the pastor, knowing the void in Richard's life and his need for a male role model, had always welcomed and counseled the boy just as he would one of his own grandchildren. Richard realized that he hadn't informed the pastor about his plans beyond high school, and it was killing him inside. Richard got so red in the face with fear and embarrassment.

Finally, the time came to disclose his plans to join the Air Force. He told his mom that he had signed up when he turned eighteen, right before graduation. He told his mom that the recruiter had told him all the benefits of joining the Air Force, how he could be sent for further training to reach the respected ranks of officer, maybe even become a fighter pilot one day, that his mom would not have to worry about paying for college and other expenses that came along with it.

But his mother was worried—and very much so. She was worried about her son going to war. She was worried about him being sent to far-flung lands and how difficult it would be for her to stay in touch. She was worried as any mother of a soon-to-be-military man would be. She knew how some of her friends had to go through the pain of losing sons and daughters to the first Iraqi war of the 1990s, how some young wives had to bury their husbands too early, and how even those who came back alive had their lives turned upside down from the trauma of combat.

Richard was determined to go; after all, once you sign the recruiter's paper, there's no going back. He just had to keep reassuring his mother about the situation. He kept telling her that the Air Force wasn't like the Army or the Marines. Richard only knew the rosy picture of Air Force planes and nice-looking stations where he would like to be posted as an enlisted Airman. As much as he wanted to please his mom and do what she wanted him to do, he was very eager to leave home and see the world.

To convince her further, he shared with her the police encounter he'd had the night he'd driven her to work and how that experience had forced him to leave town, at least for some time, to avoid any more collision with the police. Richard was in tears about the humiliation he had gone through that night. He did not want to go through that ever again. Answering his own thought, he felt that as long as he was wearing the color of his skin, never say never. The police would always find a way to harass a black man in America. His mother wanted to know why he had never told her what had happened. Richard said that he did not want to worry her any more than she already was. All his mother could say was, "Good luck, son, and be safe out there."

The bigger conundrum was how to face the reverend, so Richard told his mom to arrange a private family meeting with him, the sort of meeting that congregants occasionally had with the reverend. Such meetings were not the casual type that he usually had after a Sunday brunch; they had to be scheduled with the church secretary and on the Reverend's calendar.

To the church secretary, Mrs. Clarke, the pastor's schedule was something to look forward to; as a nosy, middle-aged, gossip-loving widow, that meant she would be the first to know the newest information about the congregants' private lives. As her desk was a couple of feet away from the reverend's office, where she could easily hear everything, she was always eager to find out the next scandal in town: who was going to get divorced or for what reason, who was leaving his or her spouse, which teenage girl was pregnant and whether abortion was permitted, etc.

Even if she failed to hear what was being said, Mrs. Clarke would casually bring up a subject related to the congregant in conference with the reverend. She would, for instance, show general sympathy about whatever situation that individual was going through to get the Reverend's attention. He would then assume that she actually knew what was happening with them and the reason for their confidential meeting. Through that indirect probing, the reverend would then succumb to her inquisitive plan and hash out the whole reason as to why the congregant was there. If she had recognized her detective and secret-searching skills, she would have chosen to be a CIA agent decades ago.

So, Richard and his mother arranged the meeting with the Reverend. Richard's mother made a phone call to make the appointment. Mrs. Clarke would sometimes urge the congregants to come in person to make sure they had a pre-conference with her. Her excuse for this was to attempt to find out the reason for the conference before attending. Some congregants found that very odd and insisted that they wanted to meet with the pastor only. When Richard's mother made the phone call, Mrs. Clarke told her that it would be better if they came to see her to go over the protocol of meeting the reverend, as though they were to meet with the pope himself, and she recommended that they come a couple of hours early.

Richard's mother had heard a lot about Mrs. Clarke, and she was not having it. She made the excuse that Richard had to work, and knowing well what Mrs. Clarke was up to, she told her that they wanted to discuss with the reverend Richard's plan to join the Air Force and get the reverend's blessings. This just killed Mrs. Clarke's curiosity; she had nothing to pre-prep now, so she said, "All right, we don't want the young man to miss his work. You guys could come to meet the reverend Friday morning at eleven."

At the meeting, Richard's mom started the discussion by informing the reverend that her son was joining the military. The reverend was not particularly pleased with the news; he was of the opinion that America only sends the poor and underprivileged black young man to its wars only to have them return traumatized, if not physically maimed and mentally injured. He asked Richard why he'd chosen the service instead of college. Richard replied that he'd seen a bunch of black kids in high school who were signing up to join the military and that the recruiter said he could have a good life.

The Reverend interrupted Richard and said, "Yes, son, you might have a good life if you come back alive." Richard's mother started to cry. Reverend Higonbothom was a matter-of-fact kind of a guy. He went on and on about how they use the poor and the black as a shield when they want to go to war, but when those soldiers come back, they shoot them for no apparent reason. "If you gonna get shot anyway, you may as well stay here with your mama, son."

Richard pointed out to the Reverend that there was no use talking about it now as he had already signed up. The reverend asked which branch of service Richard was going to join, and Richard told him that it would be the Air Force. That kind of relieved the Reverend's worries, and he exclaimed, "Oh, at least you won't be in trenches, like the Army and Marines."

So, the reverend gave Richard his blessing and lectured the young lad about how to take care of himself. He advised him not to trust everyone, but at the same time not to lose faith in humanity. He also told him to take responsibility for his actions and learn a skill in the service that he one day could use to further his career and better his life after leaving the military.

The Reverend was a very wise man; he warned Richard about the temptations of youthful life, urging him to avoid succumbing to those lively temptations, to avoid pits and trenches that those of the opposite gender could sometimes leave for a young black man to fall into, especially those deep traps laid by females of certain races. The reverend was unequivocal about the existence of different justice for different races in America, even in the military. He told the young man to avoid any conflicts with anyone and always do the right thing even when no one was looking, for when no one else is looking, God Almighty is indeed looking.

The Reverend warned the young man about a danger that had put so many young black men, rich and poor, educated and illiterate, handsome and average, in jail and for a long time: women, usually white women, accusing them of rape, attempted rape, sexual battery, etc. He gave the young man a long list of dos and don'ts about this particular subject. He told him to avoid being alone with a drunken female, to always have good situational awareness, to know who is a good friend and who is not, and to stay away from troublemakers. Richard listened well and promised his mother and the reverend that he would be a good boy.

Richard went to basic training in San Antonio. BMT, or basic military training, is an eight-week program of physical and combat training required for all enlisted airmen in the United States Air Force. The training is physically and mentally demanding and starts with the receiving week, also known as Zero Week. This first week introduces the new recruits to the rules of engagement, i.e., where to eat, the military protocol, how to take care of the living quarters, and the overall requirements of new arrivals.

Also, during this period, all trainees undergo a urinalysis to check for drug use. Anyone who fails the test is dismissed and immediately separated from the military. On the final week, all trainees, who are called this since they are about to graduate as fully enlisted airmen, participate in a 1.5-mile run, which is known as "Airman's Run." This is to celebrate their hard work and tenacity and show their drill sergeants that they are ready for combat and whatever comes their way.

On the last Friday of the last week of training, parents and spouses of the graduates usually come to enjoy and participate in the graduation of their loved ones.

Richard did very well in that tough training and earned the commendation of all his trainers. He was very excited about the technical training he was able to get from his adviser: airplane technician. This meant a lot to Richard, and he couldn't wait to share the news with his mother and the reverend. Little did he know that they had planned to surprise him at graduation. As many of his Airman friends had told him weeks prior to graduation, families were invited to join the graduation celebrations. Richard knew that his mother would not be able to afford the flight for her and her son from Memphis to San Antonio, and she did not have a dependable car to drive the distance. So, he planned to take lots of pictures with his friends and co-trainees for his family to see when he got back home during liberty time off.

Little did he know, nor his mom, that the reverend had already planned to have Richard's mom, brother, and the reverend himself fly over to San Antonio to celebrate Richard's graduation. The reverend had one of his congregants who'd once run the Marines boot camp contact the administrators at the Air Force training office to extend a graduation invitation to them.

The invitation was granted; the church made arrangements to have Richard's family accompany the reverend to surprise Richard on his graduation day. Mrs. Clarke called the family and informed them that they would be flying to Texas in a week. Richard's mom was elated and could not wait. The training officer was so kind that he seated the reverend and Richard's family in the front row so Richard would see them as the trainees marched in the graduation parade.

As the ceremony began, Richard saw his mom and little brother waving and screaming, "You made it, Richard! You really did! Much more success to you!" Then he looked to the left and saw Reverend Dr. David Higonbothom with both his thumbs up and heard him say, "May God bless you, son. You made us proud. May the Almighty be pleased with you."

Richard had a week to spend with his mother before he was to fly to Dover Air Force Base for training as an airplane mechanic. He was so excited about the opportunity, which so few of his co-trainees were able to secure. He made the best of his time off and relaxed at home.

# 4

# KHALID

*"The test of our progress is not whether we add more to the abundance of those who have much; it is whether we provide enough for those who have too little."* **Franklin Delano Roosevelt.**

As the group debates what is happening in the country, Khalid has a lot on his mind; he lived through a similar situation in Africa. He is a trained family physician who did a stint in the US Navy as a medical officer on an amphibious ship. He was commissioned officer after medical school and attached to a marine carrier at Norfolk Naval Station. He is the most internationally traveled among the group and seems well informed not only of current events in the US, but internationally as well. He has been to the Middle East, East Africa, Southern Europe, Central America, and basically every continent except Australia and Antarctica. He has a family practice in Northern

Virginia.

Khalid says, "Guys, if you have ever heard of a perfect storm, if you have ever heard in the news of the last few decades that some third-world countries are going belly up, it is happening in front of our eyes right here and right now. We are in the middle of the biggest pandemic the world has ever seen, and as a country, we are doing worse than any other. We are experiencing the worst economic downturn since we all can remember, the country is divided along racial and socioeconomic rifts, and worst of all, we don't have well-intentioned leaders who could bring the country together. We have a divided government, where each side thinks the other is destroying the fabric of the country."

Dr. Khalid, who is a naturalized citizen and was born in East Africa, has experience with what a collapsed state looks like. His mother country has gone from civil war to a non-existent central government, and the main cause was poor, corrupt leadership coupled with tribalism and communal infighting. He has seen the killings and police brutality that have been taking place in America lately. He realizes the trajectory of American civil unrest is getting worse, just as it happened in some African countries.

He says to his friends, "When leaders sow the seeds of hate and disharmony, those who are already bent on hating become emboldened to act with retribution. It appears to me that man never learns from the lessons of history."

Both Elmer and Richard show a renewed interest in Khalid's story, as it relates to what is happening in America. Previously, Dr. Khalid's friends thought his international perspectives and globally oriented opinions remote and uninteresting. As Americans, they considered themselves so far away from the direct feelings of what the rest of the world was going through. They did not appreciate how societal mistrust, whether caused by tribal feuds or partisan politics, could destroy the peace and harmony of citizens of the same nation. Ever since the election of Donald Trump, the group has paid more attention to Dr. Khalid's experiences as African, not merely to hear his anecdotes about life in the third world, but to know how that life molded him, from high school to medical school and beyond in the US.

They want to hear the whole story about his arrival in the US. This time, they want to hear it all: the civil war in his mother country, the collapse of the state and the central government, and beyond. Dr. Khalid is extremely eager to share his story, especially as it relates to civil unrest and the destruction of his native country and lessons that can be learned from it. Dr. Khalid knows that by sharing what's happening in many other developing countries where human rights abuses are rampant, the group can realize that without following the Constitution to the letter, it could happen here. US citizens have the right to know what is happening in their country.

As a young man, Dr. Khalid was born into what would be considered a middle-class family. His father was a government civil servant, and Khalid went to the public schools of what was then the capital of East-Central Africa. As history has it, the post-colonial Africa of the seventies and eighties saw coups and counter-coups, with the US and former USSR pitting one African nation against the other during the Cold War. Needless to say, there was not a single democracy on the African continent in the eighties, which was when Dr. Khalid attended elementary and secondary schools.

The worst time in Dr. Khalid's life was the late eighties, when his father was arrested on suspicion of being against the policies of the dictator in charge. It was a time of fear and uncertainty, to say the least. The government paratroopers would come in the dead of night and look for men and boys in certain neighborhoods in the capital suspected of being anti-regime. The men would be taken to the central jail, where some were chosen to be executed while others were chosen to be false witnesses against the others. Young boys were usually kept in jail until their mothers paid in dollars for their release. The process continued many times. Dr. Khalid remembered how, in October of 1987, his family decided that all the young men in that neighborhood would leave before sunset to another district to stay with relatives and non-suspected friends to avoid being hunted by the secret police. Life was so difficult and uncertain from October 1987 to 1989. The anti-government rebels were getting so close to the capital that no one knew what the next day would be like.

In the remote regions, things were even worse; some clans who were more supportive of the regime fought against those who were viewed as anti-government. The regime paratroopers usually took advantage of businesses and were extremely abusive; they took cash and anything else by force.

In the fall of 1989, Dr. Khalid was in the middle of secondary school as the country was entering a full-blown civil war. Those families who were able to escape the country left either to neighboring countries or sought political asylum in countries like the UK, Canada, or the Scandinavian countries. Dr. Khalid was lucky to be sponsored by his aunt in the United States to come to Charlotte, North Carolina. He was a teenager but had the experience of a middle-aged traveler; at a young age, he had seen a lot. He left his home as a sixteen-year-old without his parents or an older sibling. However, living through the turbulence of Africa in the eighties prepared him to face the unknown world of the Americas and all the obstacles it presented. He could speak very little English, just enough, perhaps, to be friendly, words such as "hello," "thank you," and "please," delivered with an affectionate African smile. That was it.

His first six months at an affluent, all-white American high school were not easy (only three percent of the student body was black, and two percent Hispanic). The language and cultural differences had to be overcome. He was placed in an English-as-a-second-language program with some Hispanic-speaking students from Peru, Costa Rica, Cuba, El Salvador, and Honduras. There were a couple of Japanese students and one from Spain. The English language training was planned to last for one year, by which time, students would start mainstream English in the eleventh grade. It was more difficult for Hispanic speakers to get the hang of the English Language. They spoke their own language at school and at home. It took them the whole year, and some even longer, to finish the program; however, the non-Hispanic students, including Khalid, were able to be promoted to the next level within five months.

Knowing where he came from, the civil war, the destruction, and the fact that many of his cohorts, family, friends, and classmates, were not able to get out of that horrible existence, failure was not an option for Khalid. If he didn't do so well on one test, he had to make it up on the next one to make sure that he had a good shot at getting into a good college after high school. Failing and letting his aunts and uncles who'd brought him from that godforsaken place down was the worst thing that could happen.

While in high school, he participated in international organizations such as the school chapter of Amnesty International, the Model UN, and the International Student Organization. Having witnessed brutal abuse by those in power at such a young age, he fully supported the works of Amnesty International and the United Nations High Commission for Refugees.

While pursuing his high school diploma, Dr. Khalid had to think ahead and start saving for his college expenses. As an I-20 student with no other legal immigration status, he was told that he would not qualify for student financial aid while in college. This information was extremely valuable to him and was provided by a very caring guidance counselor, Ms. Emma, Chilean by nationality, who also taught English as a second language and had experience helping foreign-born students who were not legally documented. She told him that a Social Security card would be required for any employment in the States. Luckily, her husband was also an immigration lawyer, and he helped Khalid navigate the application so the clerk would not place the hated "Unable to Work in the USA" on the back of the Social Security card.

After Khalid filled out the application, Ms. Emma took him to the county seat to acquire the card. Once Khalid had the card in hand, Ms. Emma also contacted the high school's office for youth employment services. This office, affectionately referred to as the YES office, helped high schoolers attain summer jobs to save up for a car and things of that sort.

However, in Dr. Khalid's case, getting a job after school and during winter holidays and, of course, the long summer months was for saving up for college and sending money back home to Africa to assist his family as the civil war had started right after he'd left in 1989. His first job was at a local pharmacy as a stock boy. The minimum wage was $4.95 per hour at that time. While living with relatives in high school helped greatly with room and board, he continued to save up for college. Working at the pharmacy introduced him to medicine and health care in general.

During his junior year, he decided that he would pursue pharmacy as a major in college. He regularly conversed with the registered pharmacist to find out how he'd become interested in the profession of medicine dispensary. Three pharmacists worked in different shifts. The oldest gentleman, whose name was Gregory, was a tall, blonde, red-faced sixty-something-year-old of Russian extraction; he was very keen about why this kid from Africa was so interested in pharmaceuticals and what type of medications were for what. Khalid was always very curious to know how mixing different agents would create a certain compound that would eventually heal someone's ailment. The senior pharmacist, Gregory was very kind and would explain to him how some chemicals couple together to create a new element that will be a medicine if combined with others, but could also be poisonous if taken separately; however, due to age, occasional impatience, and a taste for the vodka, which he always replenished from the Japanese liquor store next door, he would snap at times and tell the young African, "Boy, who the hell do you think I am, your chemistry teacher? Get the hell out of here and go to work. I am not paying you to teach you."

The other two guys were family men, and they were more approachable: Joe, who was Italian American, and Paul, a Polish American from Chicago. They would tell Khalid that if he was really interested in pharmacy as a career, he should excel in chemistry and biology. They stressed that he finish AP-level classes with high marks, as pharmacy school was very competitive. They also suggested that the entrance exam was very crucial to getting in. Khalid had no idea what AP classes were at that time; in retrospect, he thought just being away from all that civil unrest and fighting in Africa was enough advanced placement.

To get a different perspective, one from someone who was actually in pharmacy school, Khalid befriended a young second-year pharmacy student, Sophia, from the University of North Carolina. Sophia worked at the same pharmacy as a technician. For several reasons, she had more in common with Khalid than the rest of the employees at the pharmacy. She was an immigrant from Lebanon, another third-world country that had gone through a brutal civil war caused by sectarian conflict. She'd also left her family as a teenager to pursue an education in America. She spoke Arabic, which Khalid also spoke, as he had attended Egyptian school as a young boy.

Khalid asked Sophia how she liked pharmacy school and if her decision to become a pharmacist was the right choice. Because of their commonalities, Khalid was not shy about asking all the questions he needed to make sure that he got valuable information. Fortunately, Sophia understood exactly what Khalid was going through. She described how her older brother sponsored her to leave Beirut at a very difficult time, when the Lebanon war was at its worst. She finished high school, and since her brother was already a practicing pharmacist, she followed in his footsteps. Sophia shared with Khalid how difficult it was to finance her college education as a non-immigrant student. She said that while her brother helped her some, she basically supported herself with savings from her job as a pharmacy tech. She worked as a tech for two years before college. Khalid knew that he would be in the same boat in a couple of years and that he needed to save up money.

In his last two years of high school, Khalid made sure he got good grades in all courses, especially science and math. Graduation from high school was a momentous occasion; Khalid graduated with honors and was accepted to several colleges.

College was fun, but fun was not to be had, as Khalid needed to work over twenty hours per week with a full credit load. As was required for any pre-health science major, the core prerequisite classes were to be completed in the first two years if one was to apply for the limited pharmacy spots in the second year of college. Working and juggling lectures and lab classes was a difficult task, not to mention financial management and trying to pay bills at the age of nineteen.

Khalid's next-door neighbor in his apartment complex near campus was named Travis, and he was from New York City. By the time Khalid moved into the apartment, Travis had already been at the university for over five years and still had not graduated. At the beginning of each month, the building secretary used to knock at the door to the apartment and ask Travis, "Hey, Travis, where the hell is your rent check? Don't tell me that this time your father was late with mailing the check. You never pay your rent on time, man. I'm gonna have to take you to court. Why can't you pay your rent on time like Khalid does? He is much younger than you but more responsible. Oh, my, these American kids, man." She would always shake her head before leaving.

One day, Travis asked, "Hey, Khalid, how did you learn how to be so organized and responsible, man? You are managing your financial affairs so well at such a young age, man. I've been here for over five years and can't even finish a social work degree, man."

As Travis vented about his state of affairs, Khalid just stood there, listening. The phone rang, but Travis was not in the mood to answer it, so Khalid did, as, in those days without cell phones, the apartment phone was shared. It was Travis's dad, calling from New York. He greeted Khalid and commended him for the responsible young man that he was said to be by Travis, who, apparently, had been talking to his parents about Khalid. Khalid thanked the old man and passed the phone to Travis. They talked about something related to a rent check that was coming very late. Travis told his dad that the building manager had just been complaining about how the rent was always late.

To politely answer Travis's inquiry, Khalid told him that since he had no parents to guide him and to come to the rescue, he had to do everything for himself and out of necessity came invention. After getting to know Travis and many of his friends, Khalid came to know why so many of them did not graduate from college beyond the four years allotted for the normal first degree. Since they all qualified for financial aid with student loans and grants, some of Travis's friends continued to change their majors, which kept the loan money coming as each change increased the number of required courses. That was why it had taken Travis over five years to graduate: the tap for student loan money kept running. You see, the loan came from the Department of Education, serviced by a private bank where a high interest rate would accrue money. The university was paid by the bank, so it was incentivized to keep kids who were oblivious to their financial detriment on the hook for decades to come. The sad story was that Khalid could not even get a small loan for one class because of his immigration status, while others spent that money on beer and parties.

One night, Khalid and Travis were sitting in the living room, watching a show. Khalid asked Travis, "Hey, Travis, since you inquired about my affairs, it is only fair that I do the same tonight."

Travis said, "Go ahead, man."

Khalid asked Travis, "So, if you don't mind me asking, are you doing your master's in social work?"

Travis answered, no, he was still working on his first degree. He mentioned that his initial major was psychology, but his friends were all doing social work, and he wanted to change to it, too. He spent most of the first two years of college partying, and by the time he got serious, he realized he needed to change.

Khalid told Travis how these colleges were not looking out for the best interest of students at times, that they all wanted to get paid through loans that would be a financial burden for decades to come and that the reason they made students, especially students of color, continue to change majors was that they were milking them and their parents while failing to get them ready for the job market. Khalid advised Travis that now that he was close to the finish line for his social work degree, he must stick to it and perhaps continue with a master's.

After one semester, Travis was able to graduate and move back to New York.

Khalid continued to struggle financially. The only way to pay for his classes was to work all summer, close to seventy-five hours between two different jobs to save up enough to pay for the coming fall classes. Despite the challenges, he was able to fulfill the requirements for applying to pharmacy school. Unfortunately, the four-year college degree that was to grant a Bachelor of Science in Pharmacy was changed midstream to a Pharm-D, or Doctor of Pharmacy. This was a pure business decision for pharmacy schools to keep kids paying for an extra three years just to become pharmacists. In many students' opinion, this was just robbery of students and parents, who had to pay extra tuition and fees while the extension did not add any skill for the common local pharmacist. It negatively affected those students who were financially in difficulties to begin with. Many students had to change their plans and majors because they'd never envisioned going to school for more than the four years they'd initially signed up for.

Khalid was one of those disappointed students. He had to decide what to do. Changing majors to something completely different was not an option, as that would mean losing many credit hours, which he certainly knew how hard it was to pay for. Khalid had to make the best economic sense; he went to look at the university catalog of majors to find the closest one to pharmacy that would allow him to graduate in four years, find employment, and was still in health care. He came across nursing. Nursing was in demand, and he had already exceeded the number of credits required to attend nursing school, which was part of the same university. All he had to do was send in the application. The only small issue that was kind of in the way was that nursing was considered a female profession. Obviously, that was a chauvinistic idea, one Khalid did not subscribe to. To him, opportunity was just that: opportunity. As the saying goes, a poor man cannot be choosy.

So, Khalid decided to start the application for nursing school. The application process was very smooth; with his good grades, he was more than qualified and was accepted without reservation. He became the only male student in his class of twenty-five. He did well and got along with students and faculty members. As he excelled both in patient care and didactic courses, his professors wanted him to specialize and apply for a master's degree before he even graduated. What Khalid had in mind, something he'd never shared with anyone, was to pursue admittance to medical school and specialize in internal medicine.

Khalid's diplomacy had served him very well. Traveling across the world as a young teenager, coming to a different land with a different language and culture had taught him how to keep his cards close to his chest. He did not want to disappoint the professors who had given him the opportunity to enroll in nursing school, who had put their faith in him by offering admission to the graduate school before anyone else in the class. So, without declining the offer, Khalid showed his appreciation to the faculty. He continued to work outside school hours to support himself and pay for nursing school expenses, as he was still unable to gain the immigration status that would allow him to get loans and financial aid.

Despite the financial difficulties, Khalid graduated with high honors and received his Bachelor of Science in Nursing. He was also able to get his practicing license. Khalid got his first nursing job at a local hospital in Virginia and practiced for the next five years. During that time, he got married and started raising a family. For the most part, he was content with his profession. He started working at a private clinic, under an internist. During that time, he gained valuable experience in the area of internal medicine, where he was leaning toward specializing after medical school.

One day, as Khalid was evaluating a patient for the doctor, an idea hit him. He was sort of talking to himself and at the same time answering himself. He asked himself, "Will I ever pass this ceiling above my head? Will I ever earn more than my boss? Definitely not." To Khalid, at the time twenty-seven years of age, married, and with kids, the fork in the road had appeared. He was earning good money to maintain his family, but he could either keep at it and avoid the uncertainty of changing horses midstream or apply to medical school and face whatever the future held for him. Khalid could at the least try to apply to medical school; there would be only one of two outcomes: he got in and went for it, leading to decreased earnings in the short run but eliminating the regret that he'd never dared to try, or he didn't get in, but at least he tried and still had a good career and means to support his family.

He went home that night to discuss the idea with his wife. She was very supportive and encouraged him to go for it at full speed. She told him that he already had the patient care and bedside manners down as a practicing nurse for the last several years. The only things Khalid needed to sharpen were his study skills and getting ready for the MCAT, the Medical College Admission Test.

So, Khalid became a student all over again. It was not easy for multiple reasons. First, competing with kids who had just graduated from college the year before was tough. He had to put in extra time and longer nights. Second, he had kids at home who required the usual care of homework and doctor's visits. Third, Khalid still had a mortgage and car payments. All those obstacles notwithstanding, Khalid went ahead and started medical school.

After whatever savings he had were spent during the first two years of medical school, he had to come up with a solution to continue and finance his education. All along, he had been working at a local hospital as a locum nurse, plus summers and holidays to earn extra cash, but he did not earn enough to pay for a private medical school with very high tuition and fees. What was never an option for Khalid was quitting. He was going to finish medical school no matter what. Many of his friends and relatives were not keen about him going back to school while maintaining a family and dealing with a mortgage and other expenses related to life in America. Khalid, however, had a plan ahead of him, and with the will of God and the support of his wife, he was not going to be discouraged.

Needless to say, halfway through medical school, the money ran out. Khalid heard through other friends that the US military had a program where health care students could get scholarships and the Department of Defense would select future doctors, dentists, nurses, and psychologists as officers. Those selected would have their tuition and fees paid by the government; they would also get a monthly stipend of a modest six hundred dollars a month. The agreement stated that for each year the government paid the student's tuition and fees, the student would owe a year of service as an active-duty officer.

Khalid found this offer the only viable option for him to continue his education. He spoke with several students who had signed up for the deal, and they told him that it was a no-brainer to consider this route, especially if there were financial hardships. Khalid was the type of person who always deliberated every decision he was going to undertake. He wanted all sides of the story and the pros and cons of being in the Military. He wanted to speak not only to students who were currently in the program, which was called the HPSP (Healthcare Professional Scholarship Program), but also those who had completed the training and were now commissioned officers and practicing health care while in uniform. He spoke with officers in all different branches of the military: Air Force, Navy, Army, and US Public Health Service. They all told him that the decision they'd made was the right one. Furthermore, they said that the hands-on experience they had gained while active duty was immeasurable, the skill and confidence they had taken with them both in and out of service. They also pointed out that many in active duty did their time, usually twenty years, and were still young enough to go onto private practice, where they had two incomes: a pension from the military and a full career in the private sector.

They were more than convincing at that point, so Khalid decided to go for the formal application and contacted the Air Force. He had been informed that the Air Force was the most responsive. During that period, Khalid had only permanent residency and was awaiting his citizenship. To get the scholarship, one had to be a US citizen, so Khalid had to consult with an attorney to see if his case could be accelerated. The attorney was able to secure a court hearing where an immigration judge would hear the case to decide how soon the citizenship could be granted. The judge, after looking at the history of this young, productive, tax-paying, and law-abiding man, decided that Khalid was the epitome of the kind of successful immigrant America needed, and he granted the request to expedite the citizenship process.

In the meantime, Khalid heard from the US Navy, which offered him a two-year medical school scholarship plus additional post-grad training. Since the Air Force was not forthcoming with their offer soon enough, Khalid accepted the deal from the Navy. He was informally assigned as a US Navy ensign. The monthly stipend, though small, was helpful in paying some family expenses; Khalid still had to take loans to close the gaps on bills.

Through his friends who had already gone through the process of military indoctrination, Khalid learned about wearing a uniform, dining etiquette, salutations, and other aspects of military culture. On one occasion, Khalid and other health care scholarship recipients were invited to tour the Navy carrier, the USS *Ronald Reagan*. He drove to the largest naval station in the world, the Norfolk Naval Base in Norfolk, Virginia. There, Khalid boarded a US ship for the first time. The tour guide, a seasoned Navy senior chief of eighteen years, was teaching the soon-to-be naval officers the culture of the Navy and telling them the many hilarious encounters he'd had with many new officers.

The senior chief recalled one time when there was a new lieutenant who was coming on board as a nurse practitioner. He said she did most of the Navy etiquette of coming on board the ship by first saluting the flag and asking the officer of the deck for permission to come aboard. As the permission was granted, she came up to the flying deck of the carrier, where, at that particular moment, an ensign pilot was about to take off. As he saw the outranking lieutenant, the ensign had to salute; the young new lieutenant did not return the salute, which delayed the ensign pilot from taking off. The navy etiquette dictated that the lower-ranking officer had to hold his hand up for salutation until the senior officer returned the salute. At this moment, time was of the essence, and the pilot had to take off, so the senior chief grabbed the hand of the lieutenant to return the salute on her behalf so the pilot could take off. The ensign was much relieved and gave the senior chief a thumbs up in thanks for his assistance in the matter.

Another anecdote that the senior chief shared with the touring group was how the new officers on board tended to "over-salute" when on the ship and not wearing hats. The Navy tradition was that you don't salute indoors and when not wearing a Navy hat. The tour was very educational and useful for the group.

With his experience as a nurse, Khalid was able to do very well in his last two years of medical school, where patient care and clinical rotations took the meat of the medical training. He was so capable and excellent in-patient care that he was selected to lead clinical and hospital rotations on behalf of the attending physicians, and patients were more at ease with his receding hairline, which set him apart in age from the other students.

Khalid graduated from medical school with distinction and was immediately commissioned as a lieutenant in active duty, United States Navy Medical Corps. He took the oath with his wife and children by his side. His first active-duty Navy billet was to attend the six-week-long Naval Officer Indoctrination School at the naval station in Newport, Rhode Island. During that training, the new officers were trained in the traditions of the armed forces, how to formally dress up and dine and the ranks and responsibilities of each force.

One of the unique attributes that make the Navy different from other forces is that all other branches of the armed forces have similar rank titles. For instance, Marine, Army, and Airforce O-3 officers are called captains and have two silver bars on their shoulders. For the Navy, the rank of O-3 officer is called lieutenant. For flag officers or starred officers, the other three branches call their rank general, whereas, in the Navy, it is called admiral. So, all these titles and ranks differentiate the Navy from the other branches.

In addition to the tradition and history of the military, the officer training school was intended to introduce a routine way of life to the new officers, with exercise, marches, swimming, and lectures on the history of the United States Navy. The significant role of the Navy during World War II was revisited. The battles in the Pacific Theatre, such as at Midway, which allowed the US forces to be on the offensive, was taught to the new officers. Other notable battles included the Battle of Guadalcanal in the Solomon Islands and New Guinea, the Battle of Wake Island, the Battle of the Coral Sea, and the Battle of Attu.

After successfully completing officer training, Dr. Khalid was assigned to attend the Naval Medical Center in San Diego to get ready for being a medical officer on a US naval ship. This training was intended to prepare medical officers for all types of medical care for the sailors and Marines aboard the ship. These included annual exams, required immunization, minor surgeries, emergency care, and management of the readiness of the forces.

After one year of postgraduate training with a concentration in internal medicine, Dr. Khalid was assigned to an amphibious ship with over a thousand sailors and Marines. This ship was capable of allowing the Marines and their equipment to be unloaded close to shore so they could easily disembark for invasions or unload vehicles right near the beach. These amphibious vehicles were capable of functioning at sea and on shore. They were very successful in World War II and were used at the landing of Normandy. So, for the Marines to meet the needs of the US military, they had to be assisted by the Navy, and the amphibious squadrons were instrumental in the Marines' success ashore.

Dr. Khalid had so many hilarious memories of young marines on board. Between the ages of eighteen and twenty-seven, they were fearless and hungry for battle. With very little combat prospects on a huge Navy ship, they sometimes got bored. One time, Dr. Khalid was on an emergency call at the clinic when a young marine came in with a stab wound in his chest. He was bleeding yet laughing like it was fun to be stabbed in the chest. He was examined and checked for any internal injuries. The nurse asked him what happened and who stabbed him. He said he did it himself. Stunned and perplexed, Dr. Khalid asked him why he'd decided to stab himself.

The Marine replied, "Sir, me and my boys were just playing around. We had these bulletproof vests, you know, and we were wondering if they would also be knife-proof. We played truth or dare to see who was brave enough to be tested with the vest on to see if the knife would go through. I thought I was the brave one and felt that if a bullet couldn't go through the vest, a knife should not. So I tried it on myself and stabbed myself in the chest."

It was just crazy that anyone would do such a thing—only a Marine. Luckily, the wound was superficial, but it could have had a really bad consequence. If it had not been for one of his ribs stopping the knife's tip, it could have gone through his heart. Dr. Khalid told the Marine that this was a very reckless act and he could have killed himself. The wound was stitched up, the marine was sent back to his platoon, and the incident was reported to his captain.

In another incident, Dr. Khalid received a young Marine with his middle finger cut off at the middle flange. He was bleeding severely, and a medical tech held the severed digit, which was wrapped in gauze. After the bleeding was controlled, the operations officer was called to order a medivac for the Marine to be airlifted to a hospital for reattachment of the finger. As the medical evacuation process was being planned, the Marine said to the doctor, "Sir, I don't need to be transported to a hospital. The finger was not my trigger finger. I can still use my index finger for shooting. No need to order a medivac."

On one of his first deployments, Dr. Khalid had to meet the ship at one of the islands off the coast of Turkey. The ship was on its way back from a long deployment in the Middle East and the Horn of Africa. Dr. Khalid was flown from Zurich, Switzerland, to the ancient city of Rhodes. He arrived five days before the ship's port call. Since there was no exact date for the ship's arrival, Dr. Khalid could not make firm hotel accommodations for his stay in Rhodes. It was in the middle of summer vacation, and most notable hotels on the island were all booked up.

After arriving on a Friday afternoon flight from Zurich, Dr. Khalid looked around for a taxi. A number of Greek drivers, known for their aggressive approach with new arrivals, ran to him at once. Dr. Khalid chose the first that approached him. He told the driver that he wanted to check into the Eden Roc Hotel. This hotel had been recommended by some naval officers who had stayed there. The driver wanted to steer Dr. Khalid to one of the hotels owned by his friend; apparently, he got a kickback for every customer he brought. Dr. Khalid insisted on being taken to where he'd requested, the Edon Roc Hotel.

On the way to the main city center, the driver received a phone call from someone who sounded like a lady. Without telling Dr. Khalid, the driver made an abrupt turn into a hilly neighborhood, away from the city center. As a trained naval officer, Dr. Khalid had extreme situational awareness. Greece, although a NATO member, was not known to be a top-class European nation and was full of corruption. Dr. Khalid was concerned about the phone call and the change in direction, so he asked the driver where he was heading. The driver only knew very broken English, and he replied that he was going to get his lunch. That was the best way Dr. Khalid could translate what he was saying.

After an eight-minute drive up a hilly neighborhood, the driver pulled over to a small house with a lady standing in front of it. She handed him a brown bag of what appeared to be food. He took it and drove towards the city center. It was an awkward situation. In America, a taxi driver could not do such a thing and charge a customer at the same time. But knowing the culture of this place, Dr. Khalid was not going to fuss about it. He just wanted to check into his hotel and get ready to sightsee one of the most ancient places in the world.

Finally, the driver pulled into a place that looked like a one-story motel with a guy already waiting in the front. Dr. Khalid asked the driver why he was pulling in, and the driver said that this was his friend's hotel and the deal was better. Dr. Khalid had been patient all along, but at that moment, he basically lost it. He told the driver that he was paying to take him to the hotel of his choice, not the one owned by the driver's friend, that it is the customer who chooses what they want, not the driver, and that if he did not take him to Edon Roc Hotel as agreed, the police would be called. At that point, the driver understood that there was nothing to negotiate. He angrily put the suitcases back in the trunk of the car and took Dr. Khalid to the hotel of his choice.

Dr. Khalid checked into the hotel and rested a short bit. There was a lot to see in Rhodes, Greece, and he was going to take full advantage of every moment of it until the ship arrived. The list of places to see was endless: the ancient Acropolis of Lindos, the historic city center of Rhodes, Symi Island, the Palace of the Grand Master, Saint Paul's Bay, the Valley of the Butterflies, the former Turkish quarters, the Rhodes Islamic Era, and the Streets of the Knights.

The Acropolis of Lindos was one of the best attractions in the ancient city. Built on a 116-meter-high rock, the place was full of ancient battlefields, temples, and defensive walls. Next was the historic old town of Rhodes, considered a UNESCO World Heritage city, the largest ancient city in all of Europe. Rhodes is home to one of the seven wonders of the world, the Colossus of Rhodes, which was amazing to see in real life tour. Due to multiple fighting forces over the thousands of years, Rhodes has a multi-ethnic population, including Greeks, Turks, and Italians. Just as diverse as its people, the cuisine is phenomenally delicious and different. Dr. Khalid was interested in Islamic footprints in Rhodes and the remnants of the Ottoman rulers. The oddest things he saw there were worship places and mosques that had been converted into bars. Sadly, one could see the mosque domes where alcohol was being served on the counters. The Ottoman Empire lost Rhodes to Greek after World War I.

The next place to visit, on his second day in Rhodes, was the Palace of the Grand Master of the Knights of Rhodes. This castle, also known as Castello Castle, is a medieval structure, an example of Gothic construction in Greece, built by the Byzantines during the seventh century. After the occupation of Rhodes by the Ottomans in 1522, the castle was used as a command center.

After visiting most historical sites in Rhodes, Dr. Khalid received a phone message from the operations officer of the LSD ship, or the land docking ship, informing him that he should board the ship within forty-eight hours. Apparently, the ship had moored twenty-four hours before, but since there was a former president being hosted aboard the ship, the security was tight. Former President George H. Bush was touring the area on his family yacht for the summer. Having been a Navy man, #41 wanted to visit the sailors on board and reminisce about his youthful days as a naval aviator. The ship had an elaborate service day for him, with all aboard on the main deck.

Dr. Khalid boarded as the medical officer of the ship; his predecessor handed the medical department in an orderly manner. He would be one of the departmental heads of the ship, which consisted of all lieutenants, including the cheng, or chief engineer, the operations officer, in charge of planning and administration, the first lieutenant, in charge of deck, docking, and maintenance, the chaplain, who was in charge of the religious affairs of the crew, and the suppo, or the supply officer, who was tasked with food and fuel supplies and feeding the crew. All of those officers reported directly to the XO, or the executive officer, and had a daily meeting with him. Weekly meetings, usually every Monday morning, were chaired by the captain of the ship, and each department head would present his or her agenda for the week. Every Thursday evening after dinner, the officers attended an intel brief chaired by the captain and presented by the intel officers from the Operations Office.

Dr. Khalid gradually grew accustomed to the day-to-day activities of being on a ship and had the Navy culture well under his belt. From the initial transit at Rhodes, the ship sailed to the homeport of Little Creek, Virginia. The next port of call was the Strait of Gibraltar, nicknamed "the Rock." This historic rock marked the point of no return for ancient sailors. Since the New World was not discovered until 1492, the sailing boats did not pass beyond the Rock of Gibraltar, as no navigation was made past the Mediterranean.

With his traveling experience and knowledge of the area's history,

Dr. Khalid was the go-to for the story behind the Rock of Gibraltar. The chaplain, with his interest in religion, wanted to know the meaning of Gibraltar. Dr. Khalid told him that name, slaughtered by the Europeans, was correctly pronounced, "Jabalu-Tariq," meaning "Rock or Mountain of Tariq." The Europeans reinvented the name to sound like Gibraltar.

This rock was the namesake of a famous Muslim general, Tarik Ibn Siyad, who, in the era of Islamic expansion and conquest of Europe, invaded Visigothic Hispania (Spain/Portugal). It can be seen from a far distance both in the Atlantic as well as the Mediterranean Sea. In 711, the famous Berber Umayyad general crossed the straight from present-day Morocco to the Rock. It was said that after he landed in the kingdom of Isabela, he burnt all the ships and told his army that the sea was behind them and their enemy in front of them and the only option they had was to fight and conquer Southern Europe and expand the faith. That expansion went on for over seven hundred years. The Rock has continued to change hands ever since. It was a very strategic location that connected East to West, from Africa to Europe to the Americas via the Atlantic Ocean. After two world wars, the small piece of land by the Rock, which is geographically in Spain, belongs to the UK.

The crew of the ship had a great time sightseeing the Rock, the place where the Battle of Trafalgar took place, and the Moors' Castle, which was said to be the oldest structure in Gibraltar. For some young sailors, it was the last port call before returning to homeport, and they wanted to party and go nuts. The chance to eat out and take a break from the ship's food was great, but before long, the ship was steaming towards the wavy waters of the Atlantic and the New World.

As this was his first time on a Navy ship, Dr. Khalid started to acquaint himself with the realities onboard; he wanted to learn the layout of this large hotel on the water.

The crew was divided into enlisted members, who joined the military as young high school graduates rather than going to college, deciding to pursue a career in the armed forces. They usually came from poor backgrounds, and unfortunately, some were from broken homes. These kids were overwhelmingly Latino, black, and Filipino. They looked up to the minority officers for mentorship and moral support. The chiefs, who led the enlisted crew, were all whites who had no sympathy for those young sailors. It was extremely sad to see the disillusionment of these young men and women; many had left their homes to find a sense of belonging, only to be disappointed. Many of these young minds had been recruited by the Navy to join the service in exchange for a bright future and lifelong skills; however, many shared with officers that they were not provided the skills or career paths they had been promised. Many wanted to be electricians, computer experts, communications and intel specialists, and navigation and medical technicians. Most of those young sailors ended up in the kitchen, laundry, ship's deck, and mechanical room, and more than ninety percent were minority sailors. When asked if they had expressed their concerns about unfulfilled promises, they said that the needs of the Navy superseded any promise.

The officers were subdivided into line and staff officers. Line officers were those who joined the military as the fighting force and career military men and women. Their task was the full combat participation and defense of the ship. The staff officers were those who had gone to educational institutions first and later joined the Navy as commissioned officers. They were tasked with supporting the line officers in the areas of engineering, medical care, logistics, and analysis. The combat participation of those staff officers was limited to self-defense only; they were barred from taking part in any active combat or invasion.

Dr. Khalid was much closer to the staff officers, especially the chaplain. They were both experienced, well read, and well traveled. The line officers had a huge dislike for the staff officers; they resented the idea that someone would become a lieutenant or O-3 in a split second when they had to go through decades in the Navy to reach the officer level. The medical officers were hated even more because not only did they get promoted to lieutenant upon finishing medical school, but they also received annual specialty bonuses, as it was difficult to find doctors to join the military. This was really the thorn in the side of many line officers. Although they were resentful of the fact that the staff officers were getting special treatment, some were more hateful than others.

Dr. Khalid experienced this hateful behavior from a particular operations officer. As was later clarified by some, the contempt and hate from this officer towards Dr. Khalid was not limited to jealousy; it was rooted in racism and anti-Muslim sentiment. It started when Dr. Khalid performed his Friday prayers off-base while the ship was ashore. The operations officer had the same rank as Dr. Khalid and did not have any authority over him. They were both department heads, and the operations officer had no jurisdiction over any other lieutenant. It was relayed to Dr. Khalid by some junior officers that the ops was speaking ill about the doc and that the doc had too much special treatment. Dr. Khalid did not worry about this much and never confronted the ops officer.

At the officers' meeting with the XO, each department head would present anything new in their respective departments. Normally, the biggest news in these meetings came from the larger departments and those with lots of moving parts: supplies/logistics, engineering, operations, and the deck department, especially when on deployment. The medical department was the most stable, and as long as there were no medical emergencies, things were more or less the same. The operations officer always had something smart to say about medical and supplies; he jokingly asked whether anybody had died in medical this week or if they had enough bread in supplies. Incidentally, the supply department head was a Latino officer who also knew about the racist comments of the ops.

The XO was too nice, or perhaps too weak, to stop this nonsense, and the other department heads, who were all white, were either complicit or didn't care about such unprofessional harassment. To Dr. Khalid, those childish behaviors from a grown-up officer were beneath dignifying with complaints.

Things became much worse when the ship was assigned to take part in the relief efforts after the 2010 massive earthquake in Haiti. The crew initially left for deployment to the Black Sea, with transit ports into Istanbul, Turkey, and Croatia, and eventually the ship would join the Fifth Fleet in the Persian Gulf and around the Horn of Africa. Dr. Khalid was very much looking forward to adding those places to his traveling portfolio, but the humanitarian work needed in Haiti was an opportunity to help other human beings in desperate need. Due to that massive earthquake in Haiti, the ship had to head towards the Caribbean. There, the crew joined the USS Comfort in dealing with a devastating humanitarian catastrophe. Water, food, medicine, and clothes were to be transported from Florida and Guantanamo Bay, Cuba, to Haiti. Dr. Khalid and his crew had to get off the ship and provide medical care on the ground in Haiti. It was later estimated that over a quarter of a million lives were lost there.

The ship's crew had to modify their mandate to assisting with transportation of needed items to help the Haitian people. During officer meetings, the captain of the ship heartlessly opposed the idea of being in the waters of the Caribbean. It later became apparent that he felt contempt due to his utter racism against the Haitian people, who had just gone through one of the worst calamities of the century. During those briefings, the captain, an Irish Catholic from Boston who should have understood what discrimination against others for their faith and race felt like due to the history of his ancestors, looked down on the poor people of Haiti, who were dying in the thousands per day. The captain and the operations officer would tell each other in those meetings that the ship should be anchored over fifty nautical miles away to avoid the Haitian excrement in the waters of the Caribbean Sea. The captain said pointedly, "The Haitians don't have proper sanitation, and the further we are from shore, the better. Those Haitians have been in the hemisphere for over three hundred years, and they still live like monkeys."

The officers in attendance were divided into two groups. Some, like Dr. Khalid, were utterly disgusted that an officer of the US Navy and the captain of the ship would be so blatantly racist. Would he have said something like that about the docks of the Mediterranean Sea, which had been polluted for thousands of years? Now, one could argue that the governments of Haiti over the centuries had not been effective in bringing that country out of poverty and corruption, but natural disasters do not discriminate, and for anyone to fault the Haitian people for that disaster and be so heartless about the conditions on the ground was very sad.

Before that moment, Dr. Khalid had been unaware of the systemic bias and overt racism among the white officers on the ship. The operations officer might have been jealous of the staff officers, but the complicity of the ship's leadership added a whole new dimension. This racism and mistreatment of minority sailors by their chiefs brought a lot of young men and women to Dr. Khalid for symptoms of depression and dissatisfaction with being on the ship. The chaplain also saw his share of complaints from the black and Hispanic enlisted crew, who said time and again that the chiefs mistreated them and were biased against them.

The minority enlisted crew members, and all enlisted members in general, were supposed to lean on their chiefs for mentorship, support, and leadership. The young sailors had been told at boot camp that in the US Navy, honor, honesty, and doing the right thing even when no one was looking were the cornerstones to live by. What they saw was a one-sided application of those values, which were not worth the pamphlets they were written on. For instance, there were cases where male chiefs treated young, white female sailors favorably and recommended them for promotions so they could do less work. As what happened aboard the ship never stayed secret, it became known that some of those chiefs were having inappropriate relationships with those young sailors.

The black and Hispanic sailors who presented their complaints to the ship's leadership were rebuffed. Their arguments were not taken seriously, and some were even threatened with being kicked out of the Navy if they did not recant their allegations. As a black doctor and a leader to whom many of those kids confided in, Dr. Khalid saw the unequal delivery of justice and the disappointment of those impressionable young people. When they came to see him, they were depressed, upset, and did not know what to do.

As said before, some of those young sailors joined the Navy to run away from family problems in their homes. They had been promised that in the Navy, they would have a home, career, and a leg up in life. They would not be judged by their race, religion, or ethnicity; they were going to be judged by their hard work and dedication to their country.

After seeing these unfortunate situations, Dr. Khalid realized he was either naïve about the realities of the American armed forces and the overall implicit bias against blacks in general or he had given them the benefit of the doubt. As an African immigrant, perhaps his primary goal was to get the best education possible and make a living for his family. Many of the intricate social idiosyncrasies of American life were not on his radar. Survival and self-interest got in the way.

But over the decades, as the dust of busy life settled and he started to have American kids of his own who were going to be impacted as blacks in America, Dr. Khalid started to pay more attention to the situation., On the ship, Dr. Khalid now had a great window of observation, and he came to a disappointing realization about the fabric of America.

Dr. Khalid was very sympathetic to the plight of those young sailors; he could listen to their problems. For those with clinical depression resulting from the stress of unfair treatment or implicit bias, all he could do was refer them to psychiatric consultation on the base when the ship was ashore. In addition, he brought the concern to the chaplain, who was a close friend.

Though the chaplain provided counseling, the problem continued to fester. The enlisted leadership was not solving the problem, as some of them were the problem and others were looking the other way. The officers in charge of those departments where the abuse and maltreatment of minority sailors were occurring, such as the deck and operations, did not want to get involved in a situation they saw as being between the chiefs and their enlisted crew. They all turned a blind eye. The master chief, the highest-ranking member in charge of all the chiefs and enlisted crew, was being investigated for his own alleged domestic violence incident and could not be counted on for much.

After the humanitarian mission in Haiti ended, the ship was allowed to sail towards the Old World, to the Horn of Africa for an anti-piracy mission. For Dr. Khalid, this was going to be a momentous occasion. The waters of the Gulf of Aden would be as close as he had been to his native home for two decades. It was somewhat of a homecoming without being on the soil of East Africa. The most memorable transit was that of the Strait of Gibraltar, this time heading east. As those who crossed it would know, on a clear sunny day, one can simultaneously see Africa and Europe. As the ship travels east, one can see Morocco on the right and Spain on the left, with Gibraltar representing the United Kingdom. Dr. Khalid had been through this strait before and was well versed in the geopolitical importance of the gateway to the Mediterranean and the Old World.

The officer of the deck that day was the XO, who seemed rusty both in terms of his basic historical knowledge about the region as well as current events. As the ship slowly negotiated the narrow international waterway, one could see a distant mountain in Morocco with Arabic words on the side reading, "God, Country, King." The XO, who was aware that Dr. Khalid was from Africa, asked what the words meant. After explaining to the XO the meaning, the XO said that he thought Ghana did not have a king.

DR. Khalid was kind of perplexed by the XO's remark. He could not believe that the number two officer on the ship thought that the ship was sailing off the coast of Ghana. He asked the XO if he thought that this was Ghana. The XO said that yes, he thought this was Ghana. Dr. Khalid, forgetting for a moment that the XO outranked him, exclaimed, "Are you fricking out of your mind? You think we are on the west coast of Africa, and you are the executive officer of the ship? That is unbelievable."

The XO's face grew red with embarrassment. Dr. Khalid realized that he had made a mistake and an enemy out of the XO. He told him that this was the kingdom of Morocco and the northern part of Africa and that Ghana was on the west coast. The XO, a man six-plus feet tall and well built, seemed so small upon realizing that he did not know where his ship was. From that day on, the XO and Dr. Khalid did not see eye to eye, for the XO knew that it was not acceptable for a high-ranking officer to not know where his crew was.

On its way through the Mediterranean, the ship's next port of call was Rhoda; the main purpose of this port visit was to replenish supplies and fuel the ship. Due to a time crunch and the fact that the captain was very reluctant to have the crew go on liberty, the crew was stuck on board. However, with the Mediterranean Sea being lined with many historic and ancient spots, more places remained to be seen before crossing the Suez Canal into the Red Sea. Some of those Spanish enclaves included Valencia and Barcelona. Cartagena was another delightful town with many historical places. On the Italian coast, there was the opportunity to visit Sicily, Licata, and Marina di Ragusa. There was also Turkey, which the ship had missed due to the Haitian earthquake, but again, the captain was adamant about not pulling into any of those sites.

As experienced sailors along the waters of the Mediterranean commonly said, the sailing of that sea could be well settled or unsettled depending on the season. During the period the ship was heading to the Red Sea, the weather was clear, with blue sky most of the time and clear visibility. There were light winds on the western side of the Mediterranean, but that diminished as the ship headed east.

As the ship continued towards the Eastern Mediterranean, the message spread that the new plan was to pull into Alexandria, Egypt, for a couple of days and continue onto the Suez Canal by way of Port Said. The ship pulled into the Alexandria Harbor on a cool Sunday morning. For those who sail, the best way to appreciate a coastal city is to come into it by boat. The speed of the ship as it moored was slow, which was conducive to appreciative sightseeing, both close and at a distance.

Again, this was a great opportunity for Dr. Khalid to reacquaint himself with the history he'd learned in Egyptian schools he'd attended before coming to America.

Alexandria, also called the Bride of the Mediterranean by its residents, is a city of 5.5 million people and is considered by some the largest city on the Mediterranean. For a long time, it was the second-largest city and commercial point of Egypt. As the name indicates, it was founded in 331 BC by Alexander the Great.

The crew was allowed to disembark the ship, and everyone with the liberty to leave the ship had the opportunity to do so. Dr. Khalid did not waste any time, taking along the list of places to see in Alexandria and things to do. After a hearty meal, which every officer on the ship was looking forward to as they had all gotten tired of the ship's food, Dr. Khalid and the chaplain went on a scavenger hunt for Alexandria's historical landmarks. They started with the Library of Alexandria, considered one of the largest in the world. The Abu Al-Abbas Mursi Mosque, the most famous mosque in Alexandria, was another spot.

It appeared that the chaplain was not only interested in the Protestant branch of Christianity, but also comparative religion. After Rome and Constantinople, Alexandria is considered the next most significant city in Christian history. As the seat of the Roman Empire until the year 430, Alexandria has a huge number of archeological remnants of the Romans. It was only the right thing to do that the Temple of Taposiris Magna be given a visit. This temple, built in the Ptolemy era, was dedicated to Osiris. The city of Alexandria showcased all the monotheistic religions, with Eliyahu Hanavi Synagogue for the Jewish faith, Saint Catherine Church for Catholics, and different mosques and madrasas for the majority Muslim inhabitants of the city.

As the Alexandria port call was coming to an end, the arrangements to travel through the Suez Canal was being made behind the scenes, and already, after the two-day visit, the navigation team was huddling over the charts and maps of the canal. This canal connecting the Mediterranean to the Red Sea was 192 kilometers. Starting from Port Said, it ended at Port Suez. Before the completion of the canal, the ships from Europe and the Americas had to encircle the continent of Africa to reach the Middle East, the Indian subcontinent, and China. The Suez Canal connected the Mediterranean to the Middle East and the Horn of Africa. With the geopolitical changes of the area and the era, the canal had never been more instrumental in connecting the continents.

As soon as the transit of the canal started, the ship and its crew were to stay on a level of high alert. It was communicated to the crew that the area was considered a hazardous zone. That came with at least one benefit: income would not be taxed. The ship's company, especially the young lads, were warned about the cultural differences, some true and some extremely biased and on the verge of open racism. For instance, the young men were told that although the area from the Suez Canal to the rest of the Arabian Peninsula was the cradle of civilization, the people of the region were no longer civilized. The reason American ships were in the region was to bring some sense of "civilization to the barbaric and backward Arabs and Muslims." The leadership of the crew, led by the illiterate maritime executive officer, who could not tell North Africa from West Africa, lectured the crew about how backward the culture of the people on both sides of the Red Sea was. Just as they had demeaned the Haitians, they did the same thing here. None of them knew how the entire human civilization had started not far from the waters of the Red Sea. They knew nothing of the Mesopotamians, the Persians, the Arabs, the African civilizations, and the eventual Islamic conquest of Southern Europe, which brought science and mathematics to Spain and France when Europe was in the dark ages, or how some of the oldest learning centers of the world are not London and Paris but in West Africa, Egypt, and Morocco.

As the ship passed through the canal to the Red Sea, the security alert was extremely high. There were hot spots on both sides of the banks of the Red Sea. On the right side were the countries of Sudan, Eretria, Djibouti, and Somalia, all of which were considered by the

State Department to be unsafe to travel to based on the geopolitical conditions on the ground. In addition to the political and economic instability of the Horn of Africa, there was also the issue of piracy. This period saw a huge spike in piracy activity in the Gulf of Aden, the Red Sea, and the Indian Ocean.

On the left side of the sea, the hottest spot was Yemen, where the attack on the USS *Cole* in 2000 had left a bad memory. Apart from that, there was an impending civil war in Yemen between the Houthis and the pro-Saudi government in Sanaa, so alert mode was indeed warranted. What was not warranted was the despicable racial overtone spearheaded by the commanding officer and condoned by other white officers and chiefs.

Being on this ship changed Dr. Khalid's perspective on the realities of America. When evaluating race relations in American society, the armed forces had always been identified as one of the most integrated institutions. However, being in the Navy had exposed the American military's true colors. Dr. Khalid realized that if the Navy was considered understanding and empathetic to racial harmony and equality, how much worse things were in mainstream America!

The way the minority enlisted crews were treated was utterly unacceptable; their needs and complaints were not addressed, and their promotions were not based on hard work and seniority. Since all the chiefs were white, they selected their own for promotions and awards.

The ship finally anchored in the waters off the coast of Djibouti. The plan was to be on the lookout for any piracy in the Gulf of Aden and assist the Marines with their expeditionary exercises. The Marines had their equipment on the ship and had joined the ship in Djibouti. To do those exercises, the Navy had to get permission from the host country.

The discussion on requesting permission to initiate the exercise occurred in the wardroom, and the Marine commander and Navy captain went through the formal process. The Marine commander was adamant about not putting too much stock in asking permission from the host nation. He wanted to do whatever they needed to accomplish their mission. The captain of the ship, although agreeing with the Marine's disregard for the respect of the territorial waters of the host country, was more concerned with the safety of the ship and its crew. He felt it was important to gain that green light from the host African nation.

The request was sent through the proper channels; however, there was much to be desired in the speed of the response. The Marine and Navy officers, including the operations officer, did not hide their frustration about the delay. The operations officer complained that the American military should not be asking for permission to do the exercise. He said, "What the fuck these poor Africans going to do to us if we initiate the exercise without their permission?" He sarcastically answered his own question by saying, "Oh, they might use their submarines to destroy this ship." He and the other officers spoke of these sovereign African nations as though they were American colonies. The sad part of the whole discussion was that none of the officers thought that what they were saying was utterly unacceptable.

Permission for the exercise was eventually granted, and the Marines were able to land on the beaches of the Gulf of Aden with their amphibious assault vehicles. Dr. Khalid joined the exercise group to have an inside experience as to how the LCACs function. These landing craft air cushions are used as landing vehicles in the US Navy. They are capable of landing on shore while functioning as speedboats in the water. The Marines use them to transport military vehicles, weapon systems, and cargo ashore for their beach assaults. The LCACs landed very close to the beaches of Djibouti, and the Marines completed their exercise.

The rest of the deployment was uneventful, with the ship going back and forth between the Persian Gulf and the Gulf of Aden. However, the unethical behavior of the officers and chiefs continued to bother Dr. Khalid, who tried hard to stay above the fray and be as professional as possible.

The ship added an African American female chief, who was transferred from San Diego. Before her arrival, the other chiefs, who were all male, were already talking about how difficult it was going to be to have an "ABW" on the ship. Dr. Khalid overheard this from the chief in the medical department who directly reported to him. The medical department chief had a good working relationship with Dr. Khalid, but he was more loyal to his chief friends socially; he shared with Dr. Khalid all sorts of things that took place at the chiefs' table. The medical chief thought that Dr. Khalid was not really black; with his slight accent and different culture, the chief thought the doc was from somewhere in Asia. He often mentioned to Dr. Khalid that he resembled a chief from his last ship, a close friend from Sri Lanka.

Oblivious to the fact that Dr. Khalid was from Africa, the chief shared with him the most intimate stories about the other chiefs. How some white chiefs were having improper relationships with young female sailors, which, in military law, is considered sexual harassment. How those female sailors were getting preferential treatment and recommendations for commendation, promotion, and assignments to the rates of their choice. How, when some of the minority sailors complained about the unfairness of the white chiefs, their concerns were not addressed and some of them were actually punished for complaining.

Dr. Khalid listened to all of this, and when he asked why this unfair treatment was tolerated, the chief's response was that black and Hispanic sailors should be lucky to have jobs, that life was never fair so they needed to shut up or get out. Dr. Khalid asked the chief what was meant by "ABW." The chief was surprised that Dr. Khalid didn't know that it meant "angry black woman." The doctor continued to probe, asking why anybody would call someone they hadn't yet met an angry person. The chief's response was that all black women were angry, like they were owed something. Dr. Khalid thought, *If this is not racism, what is?*

Everyone was awaiting the arrival of this female chief, who was to take over the supply department. This was a huge department where the logistics of food, ship stores, mail service, and other supplies were managed.

Obviously, the male chiefs had mixed feelings about having a female in their midst. They could no longer have their chauvinistic and racist locker room talk, in their minds an inconvenience of the integrated Navy of the 21st century.

The new female senior chief was confident and ready to take her position. At her previous post at the Naval Support Center in San Diego, she had been a true leader and mentor for her crew. She had been involved in training and leading the supply department, and she'd chosen to be deployed at sea to increase her chances for promotion to master chief. Her name was Nicole, and she had the composure and confidence to get what she wanted, and no one was going to stop her.

Perhaps the white male chiefs were threatened by her achievements and goals, which they must have read about in her bio prior to getting the orders. Had those male chiefs been decent men of honesty and integrity, they would have felt happy about the addition of a successful female chief, which would only increase the success of the ship. They would have realized that the opinion of a female chief was a plus for the command's future. They were not visionary at all; they only felt threatened by her, and their insecurity was extremely transparent.

As soon as Senior Chief Nicole joined the ship, she took control of her department. She shared with her enlisted crew that she was going to be mentoring them, looking out for their best interests, and listening to their concerns. The crew was delighted to hear that a chief cared about their complaints. As most of those sailors were minorities, they were excited to know that things were not going to be the same now that the new senior chief, a black female, would be at the helm.

Some of the enlisted crew in the supply department were transferred from the other departments of the ship as rotational crew. Among them were some female sailors who had initially worked in the deck department, where most complaints among the minority sailors originated. Those young female sailors saw in Senior Chief Nicole a great sense of empathy and sensitivity to their concerns. They told her what was happening in many other departments and how the black, Hispanic, and Asian sailors were discriminated against by the white chiefs, how their concerns had been overlooked to the point where they had been threatened by punishment and removal from the Navy. The senior chief was very upset about how those young women were treated; she told them that no one was above the law and, moving forward, she would do anything to help them. However, whatever happened before her arrival, she could not undo.

During her transition, the senior chief noticed that she was not getting the collegial support and welcome that chiefs normally extended to one of their own. The other chiefs were giving her the cold shoulder, and she felt very lonely on the ship. This unusual treatment got worse when the white chiefs found out that she was mentoring the enlisted females on their rights and harassment. The story went throughout the ship like wildfire. Even the young white female sailors who saw the injustice and abuse came forward with their complaints and sought advice from the senior chief.

A nineteen-year-old deck girl came forward and reported that her chief had been forcing himself on her ever since she'd come on the ship more than eight months ago. When she rebuffed his advances and informed him that what he was doing was wrong and against the rules of the military, he sent her to perform the hardest and worst types of work and denied her liberty and vacations. When she reported the issue to her immediate superior, he told her that chiefs ran the ship and she needed to get in line to get along. This young lady also pointed out to her new mentor, Senior Chief Nicole, that many young ladies had told her that they were leaving the Navy altogether because of similar mistreatment.

The senior chief had no choice but to bring this up to her department head. She informed him that many young ladies were coming to her, complaining about sexual harassment by their chiefs. The department head told her that there had been some complaints before her arrival but they had been found to be untrue and she should not get too involved in unproven allegations. The senior chief told her department head that, with all due respect, she had a duty to stand up for what was right and if there was any suspicion that any female on the ship felt harassed, there should be a full investigation. She asked the lieutenant whether there was a sexual harassment prevention program and if anyone was assigned to the post. The department head told her that he was not aware of a post that dealt with that issue and, if there was, it would not be in the supply department. The senior chief said she would bring the subject up in her next meeting with the master chief.

The weekly meeting among the chiefs took place in the command master chief's office. The normal discussion went as usual, and no one had additional business to discuss. Senior Chief Nicole said that she needed to bring up an issue that was not going to be popular: the ship needed sexual harassment prevention training. She pointed out that this would be a great educational subject for the young sailors, who could benefit from the training. She underlined that with young men and women of different ranks on the ship for extended periods at sea, it would behoove command to teach them the importance of consent and how to prevent running into trouble.

The male attendants in the meeting looked at each other, communicating in an unspoken way, "I told you so." The master chief interjected and said that it was a good idea and command leadership would have to discuss the recommendation further. He also promised to bring up the subject with the captain.

In the days immediately after the meeting, Senior Chief Nicole was ostracized and excluded from social meetings and games. The all-male chief's mess made the point that she was not welcome. She did not take it as badly as they would have liked. She continued to do her work and mentor the crew the best that she could.

After several weeks of waiting to hear back from the master chief, she was informed that the captain did not feel it was necessary to have sexual harassment prevention training for the crew, and if anyone on the ship were accused of such a thing, they would need to be brought to leadership's attention. The senior chief felt defeated; she could not get any support from her superiors, and at the same time, the female sailors' complaints continued to be ignored. She was relentless, however, in documenting any concern presented to her by her crew or their friends in different departments.

Next, she approached the medical department. She knew that Navy protocol was to reach out to her counterpart chief there, but she also knew that all the chiefs were on the same side and he was not going to bring up these issues with Dr. Khalid. So, she directly approached the doctor and told him that the young female sailors being harassed and mistreated when they didn't comply with advances was having a negative effect on their readiness. She pointed out that some of the girls were showing signs of extreme depression and a few had shared that they'd had suicidal thoughts.

The doctor was alarmed at how dangerous this issue was going to be if command did not address it head on. He told the senior chief that he would consult with the chaplain to see how the issue could be addressed at the next officers' meeting.

Dr. Khalid and the chaplain had a long, frank discussion about the situation, and although both knew how endemic the problem was, they both had no quick way to fix it. It was always left to the command master chief, who, in turn, only looked out for his chiefs. But as the issue of suicidal thoughts among the female sailors had surfaced, it was important to bring it up. They both agreed that they needed to let the XO head this matter and let the CO decide how to nip it in the bud.

The chaplain brought up the subject to the XO at the department heads' meeting. He started by saying, "There have been long-standing complaints among the enlisted females in some departments. Some of these complaints have been investigated before, but the medical department is getting more serious medical complaints stemming from alleged sexual abuses and harassment from some members in the chiefs' mess. Some of these sailors have been extremely depressed and have sought both clerical counseling as well as medico-psychiatric intervention. If we don't address these issues, they will come back to haunt command."

Dr. Khalid took over after the chaplain and reiterated that it was an absolutely serious matter when a sailor on deployment and thousands of miles away from their family and support system has to face these types of problems but their superiors, who were supposed to support them, were not addressing their concerns. Dr. Khalid pointed out that some of these young ladies had already lost confidence in the promises made by the Navy, that they needed to be protected before it was too late.

The operations officer took over and told the XO that this whole thing was being blown out of proportion and these young ladies had nothing to complain about. Dr. Khalid interjected and slammed the idea that the victim was being blamed. He told the operations officer to stay within the limits of his job, that the chaplain and the medical departments were tasked with the well-being of all sailors aboard the ship and, by bringing forth the concerns of those female sailors, they were doing their jobs.

The head of the deck department, where most of the complaints had come from, asked if there were any new complaints from his department. Dr. Khalid told him that this was beside the point, that command needed to have a blanket policy to address the issue of harassment and treat those affected by it. The XO intervened and said that any type of harassment was unacceptable and he would discuss the matter with the captain.

The XO brought up the subject at the weekly command department head meeting. The captain started by saying that the XO and respective department heads should develop a plan to further investigate the issue and train sailors about sexual harassment. Dr. Khalid stressed the importance of coming up with a treatment plan for those affected by the bad experience. Since the ship was on deployment and there was no psychiatrist on board, it was hard to treat those sailors who were severely depressed and showed signs of suicidal ideation. The doctor suggested that they pull into the closest port to seek psychiatric treatment for those sailors. The ship was anchored deep in the Indian Ocean at the time, and the closest medical facility was Camp Lemonnier Naval Expeditionary Base.

The XO promised that he was going to bring up the suggestion to the commanding officer to plan a port visit to the camp so that sailors in need could be sent to the clinic there for psychiatric evaluation. The captain did not see any urgency in arranging a port visit anytime soon;

he did not want to deviate from the ship's training plan.

Dr. Khalid continued to see the sailors concerned on a weekly basis to make sure that they were doing okay. He also requested that those sailors were not to stand watch or handle any firearms. He could not offer them any treatment since they had not been evaluated by a psychiatrist. What he was not aware of, and what the sailors did not bring up to anyone, was the bullying and abuse that followed their complaint. The male chiefs used their enlisted underlings to abuse the girls who had complained. Since most of their past concerns were never properly addressed and since they were punished for speaking out, they stayed quiet and internalized their grief.

Four weeks later, the ship's training schedule took it to fifty nautical miles outside Djibouti. Dr. Khalid had already arranged with the psychiatrist to evaluate five female sailors: two who had expressed a history of suicidal thoughts and three who were clinically depressed. The Marine helicopter was to take Dr. Khalid, one of his medical technicians, and the five sailors to Camp Lemonnier Medical Clinic.

At 8:45 on a Wednesday morning, Dr. Khalid changed his navy uniform to summer khakis, since he was going ashore. The medical technician was a twenty-four-year-old male from Mississippi. He was to gather the sailors for the helicopter ride to the clinic. Dr. Khalid was ready to take in the experience of being on the soil of his home; Djibouti is a majority Somali city. Being there was the same as being in his homeland of Somalia after twenty-one years, so he waited for the sailors to meet him in the medical department.

The helicopter was to take off at no later than 9:30, but at 9:00, Dr. Khalid was still waiting, and there was no sign of the sailors. He asked the medical chief to radio the medical technician, who replied that he was outside the ladies' room, waiting for one of the girls to come out. He waited ten minutes more. At that point, Dr. Khalid was very concerned. He asked which girl they were still waiting for. When the technician told him the name, he told the medical chief to bring his emergency kit, and they ran to the enlisted female quarters.

There, Dr. Khalid ordered the door to the bathroom broken open. Once it was open, they rushed in and found that the young female sailor had used her belt to hang herself. The doctor checked her; there was no pulse, no breathing. The bridge was called to sound the emergency alarm, and the medical staff brought the body to the medical department for proper documentation.

The captain called for an emergency meeting with all the department heads to discuss the tragedy. The deceased sailor was a twenty-one-year-old white female, formerly from the deck department; she had been transferred to the supply department and had been serving in the officers' wardroom. Many of the officers knew her very well.

The captain started the somber meeting with a sad tone, as would be expected in such a terrible situation. He asked the chaplain to say a prayer. The plan for informing her family and burial at sea, if ok with her next of kin, was discussed. Dr. Khalid requested that a suicide watch be placed on the other four sailors and that their clinic visit planned for the next day. The captain approved the doctor's request and asked him and the chaplain if sending the sailors sooner could have saved the dead sailor's life. The chaplain replied that it might well have, but he added that if command had addressed the young female sailors' concerns, as had been suggested by the supply department's senior chief, they might have all been in a better circumstance.

The captain did not care for the chaplain's insinuation that command was to blame for the death of the young female sailor. However it was to be sliced, the fact remained: had the complaints been treated with the seriousness they deserved, there would not have been a suicide. The captain knew that the medical doctor would agree with the chaplain, so he did not ask him to express his opinion.

The operations officer reported that the medivac for the other four sailors had been arranged for the next day at the same time. Dr. Khalid thanked everyone and instructed the medical staff to have the body placed in the ship's morgue. The chaplain informed leadership for the enlisted staff and anyone who had worked or was close to the deceased sailor that they could come in for counseling. The communications department was able to get in touch with the next of kin, and they agreed to the burial at sea.

The medivac arrived the next day, and the sailors were brought ashore for psychiatric evaluation. Dr. Khalid remained on the ship and told the medical staff on the helicopter to have the sailors checked into the clinic at the camp; he planned to finish up the death certificate and rejoin the sailors the next day. After a complete evaluation, the attending psychiatrist ordered the sailors admitted to the psychiatric ward for further examination. When Dr. Khalid arrived at the hospital, the attending psychiatrist informed him that the girls had shown symptoms of a severe type of post-traumatic stress disorder. Some of them had even shared with the psychiatrist how they were abused before coming to the navy and, after they were harassed and sexually assaulted, some of those horrible experiences from their past resurfaced.

The psychiatrist broke the news to Dr. Khalid that it was a miracle that more of them had not succumbed to suicidal urges. The psychiatrist suggested that the girls needed to be under his direct observation for a week and, when he deemed them seaworthy, they would have to undergo long-term counseling at a psychiatric health care facility. Both Dr. Khalid and the attending psychiatrist agreed that returning the girls to the ship would, at the least, trigger new episodes of depression, especially when they remembered their friend who had taken her own life. Therefore, it was best that the girls stay ashore until their long-term prognosis was assured.

Dr. Khalid returned to the ship via Marine helicopter and told command leadership that there was no way for the girls to return to the ship without a relapse of depression and mental breakdown. He suggested that the girls be officially transferred to Camp Lemonnier as their home base until they got better or were medically discharged. Furthermore, Dr. Khalid added, they must initiate a full legal investigation of what led to the sailors' depression, especially the sexual assault and bullying that followed after they complained about their mistreatment. In fact, the bullying and harassment of the girls, perpetrated by their peers at the instigation and order of the chiefs who were being reported, was the straw that broke the camel's back. They were mistreated and abused by their superiors, and when they complained, they were further punished and bullied.

The command master chief did not want his reputation to end this way, but he could not undo what had been done.

The psychiatrist caring for the four sailors at the Navy clinic in Djibouti called Dr. Khalid to update him on their condition. He reported that two of the girls were responding well to treatment; however, the other two had experienced continuous relapses of suicidal thoughts. Furthermore, one of those had made a suicide attempt. The doctor suggested that in light of the trauma suffered by the girls, he was recommending a full medical discharge for at least two of them, followed by continuous care at a veteran's psychiatric care in their home states.

Back on the ship, the burial plans continued; the entire crew stood on the ship's flight deck to take part in the sending off of their fellow sailor. The pain was more visible among the young enlisted females who had worked with the deceased. As relayed by the chaplain, whose department was tasked with counseling and caring for the friends of the deceased, the morale of the ship's enlisted crew had never been lower. The minority female enlisted crew, in particular, could not wait to leave the ship. They felt used and abused by their chiefs and that their complaints remained unaddressed. The chaplain lamented that it had to take the death of an innocent young sailor for command to realize the danger of bullying and sexual and racial harassment and the ramifications of not treating all individuals equally.

The master chief started the process of medically discharging the four sailors, and after several weeks, life came back to normal on the ship, never mind investigating the circumstances surrounding the death of the sailor and the cause of her suicide—or finding out the reason why four young ladies had been medically discharged right after the suicide of their friend. The ship's leadership hoped things would soon return to normal.

At this time, the ship was heading up to the Persian Gulf, and after months of not pulling into a port, the plan was to have a port visit to Manama, Bahrain. This was the seat of the US Navy's Fifth Fleet. The ship was to anchor there for a week and have a change of command, where a new captain would take the lead.

Bahrain is a liberal country among the Gulf nations, bordered by the more conservative big brother Saudi Arabia. The supply officer planned an elaborate dinner party for the farewell of the captain and to welcome the new one. All officers joined the dinner party, and the event was opened by the chaplain saying some prayers. After dinner, each officer made a farewell comment to the outgoing captain. The captain then returned the favor.

As was described before, the captain was a Bostonian Catholic of Irish extraction. He was of the opinion that the only acceptable faith was the Roman Catholicism that he practiced. He started his speech by sarcastically questioning if the prayer of the infidel, the chaplain being a Protestant, was going to be accepted. Dr. Khalid knew the chaplain very well, and the two were very close, joining on their port visits and touring historic places together, and he saw how uncomfortable the Captain's comment made the chaplain feel. The chaplain was visibly upset and got very red in the face. The captain continued his rant about how he'd made the ship successful and turned things around, especially the condition of disrepair he'd inherited from his predecessor. The remarkable point he missed was that his predecessor had had no issues with his crew committing suicide because of abuse on the ship.

After the captain finished his speech without any applause or approval from the party attendees, Dr. Khalid thought he had to break the tension and awkward silence with a little humor and cheer up his friend, the chaplain. He said that he had never thought in his wildest dreams that two Christians would be calling each other infidels while a stone's throw away from Islam's holiest place, Mecca. Everybody in the room laughed hard except the captain. Ironically, at that point in time, the one who got red in the face was the captain. The chaplain, who knew Dr. Khalid to be extremely witty and daring, was having the time of his life. Dr. Khalid had answered for the chaplain and indirectly defended him against the captain, who had shown no respect for someone else's faith.

After a week of relaxation and sightseeing in Bahrain, the ship had to head back to the Gulf of Aden. The change of command with the new captain was to take place there. Somehow the captain was hoping to get off the ship before any investigations about the previous incident could start. He knew it was going to be someone else's problem. The ceremony was just a usual Navy change of command. The new captain was a very decent Midwestern guy who appeared to be down-to-earth and respectful of the other officers.

The new captain was briefed on the current situation of the ship and how things had gotten to where they were, that someone had actually committed suicide. That brief came from the commodore, who, apparently, was conducting an internal investigation. That investigation was ongoing, and the new captain was assured that it was not on his watch that the tragedy had occurred but he would let the chips fall where they may to find out the true cause of death of the young sailor and how to prevent any further upheavals on the ship.

The new captain confided in the chaplain and sought his support in the investigation. The chaplain, who had the utmost confidence in Dr. Khalid, told the latter that the commodore was not going to leave any rock unturned to bring to justice those responsible for the alleged sexual harassment that led to the death of the sailor. Knowing that the commodore's investigation would need witnesses, the captain had already identified those who were genuinely concerned about the well-being of the minority sailors, including the Senior Chief Nicole, the chaplain, and Dr. Khalid. The new captain had his plan ready.

The ship got underway to the Red Sea. The next liberty port was Aqaba of Jordan. This is where the Red Sea terminates. As the ship headed north, to the right of the Red Sea was the Gulf of Aqaba, and to the left was the Sinai Peninsula of Egypt. This was another opportunity for the crew to explore one of the most ancient places in the world.

As usual, the crew planned to have five full days of liberty on the beaches of the Aqaba Gulf. Some junior officers had rented hotel rooms at the Aqaba Inter-Continental Hotel. Since there was no alcohol allowed on American ships, as they called it a dry navy, the young sailors looked forward to having as much booze as they ever wanted in that hotel.

Dr. Khalid and the chaplain went to the beach to relax, swim, and have dinner at one of the local restaurants. Jordanian buses were rented for the crew to go to downtown Aqaba. The junior officers invited the two senior officers, Dr. Khalid and the chaplain, to join them for dinner at the one and only Inter-Continental Hotel. Neither one of them had been to that luxurious hotel, so they accepted the invitation. Everyone went to the beach, and those who had arranged hotel rooms in advance checked into their rooms for drinking and whatever else.

At the beach, Dr. Khalid and the chaplain went to a young junior enlisted African American sailor, who was enjoying himself under the sun after swimming a few laps. He felt a bit uneasy with two senior department heads coming his way, but he was told to be at ease and have fun on his liberty time.

While the chaplain and Dr. Khalid were within earshot of the young sailor, four white warrant officers, who had joined the Navy as enlisted crew but, over time, been promoted to officers, approached the pool. They called out to the young black sailor, "What are you doing here, man?" He replied that he was sun-tanning. One of the warrant officers remarked that the young black sailor was actually tanning the sun, a slight comment that could have been taken as a racist remark.

They continued laughing and carrying on with the undertone that since he was dark, there could be no need to suntan. The other three laughed very loud, and the Chaplain called them out and told them that what they'd done was unacceptable and unbecoming of officers and he would take it up with their commanders. He told them that in light of what had happened on the ship recently, they should have known better. Dr. Khalid also reprimanded their behavior.

The warrant officers said that they were only joking and the young sailor was grown up and could handle the joke. This blatantly racist behavior was rampant on the ship, and a systemic overhaul was needed to change the perception of some of the crew who were bent on hurting young minority sailors with their off-the-cuff, prejudiced verbal abuse.

Later that afternoon, the command officers had a beach party at the resort, and all department heads were invited. It had rained a couple of hours before, and the tent under which everyone was sitting had quite a bit of water on top of it. Dr. Khalid, the chaplain, and others were sitting inside the tent, while others were standing around. The operations officer came out of nowhere and flipped the tent from inside, causing the water to splash on everyone near the tent. Nobody knew whether he'd had a bit too much to drink at that moment. What he'd done was something only a child would do, so everyone was like, "What the heck?" Dr. Khalid was the only one who stood up to him and said, "When you are doing this when you're middle-aged, people wonder what you used to do as a kid in elementary school."

Oh, my, that just did it. The operations officer screamed at the top of his lungs and told Dr. Khalid, "All of you docs and chaps and whatever think you are smarter than us. It took you all couple of years to put on that stupid oakleaf Navy shit, while we had to put in over twenty years." He just kept on and on about how it was unfair that doctors and dentists got a bonus when they had to go to wars and risk their lives.

Dr. Khalid just kept his cool and told him that it was up to him to go back to school and earn those professional degrees and extra training to qualify for bonuses. "As they say in the Navy, you choose your rate; you choose your fate." The operations officer just exploded with anger when he heard that. He could not defend his argument after that, so he went back to the ship very mad. The rest of the officers cheered as soon as he left and told Dr. Khalid that it was great that he'd told the guy off. Nobody had ever told him the truth, and that was why he ran over other officers. From that day on, the ops hated Dr. Khalid, but he sure got the hell out of his way.

As was planned, some of those same warrant officers and other junior commissioned officers were to have house parties in the hotel rooms. However, Dr. Khalid and the chaplain were not into all that. After a long day of swimming, they wanted to get ready for dinner. Dr. Khalid needed a place to change and shower, and the ship's combat system officer, one of those who had rented a room in the hotel, offered the use of his room to shower and change.

So, Dr. Khalid went up to the room to change. When he entered the bathroom, he walked in on one of the warrant officers about to take his liberty with a much younger enlisted sailor. Dr. Khalid told him to stop it right there. He ordered the officer to get dressed and get out of the room. He asked the young lady if she was hurt or anything. She replied that she was fine, and after dressing, she walked out and yelled at the warrant officer that they could reconnect another time. Had Dr. Khalid not caught them in the act, it would have been too late.

As soon as he changed clothes, Dr. Khalid received two emergency phone calls. One was for a young Native American enlisted sailor who was inebriated after a long night of drinking. Dr. Khalid performed CPR and stabilized him before contacting the Jordanian Army Hospital in Aqaba. The other call concerned a rape attempt by one of the chiefs. Dr. Khalid informed the chief's department head about the situation, and the victim was taken to the local hospital.

Contrary to the hope that things were going to get better, the problems had gotten out of hand. The chaplain and Dr. Khalid returned to the ship and reported everything that occurred at the hotel to the XO. They stressed that a full investigation be undertaken and that if the ship's new captain did not make tangible changes and the alleged abuses were not confronted, they were going to have more problems.

The news created the first emergency meeting of department heads with the new captain. The new commanding officer broke the news to all present that he had been aware of the tragic death that had occurred on the ship; he had been briefed by the commodore's staff. He told the officers that he would stick to his guns and find out who was responsible for the previous offenses as well as the more recent incident that took place at the Inter-Continental Hotel.

The previous captain created a committee led by the chaplain to put out the fire in an attempt to keep the issue within command. However, there was no way of keeping the death of a sailor on the ship secret. The report had to be sent to the commodore of the squadron. The commodore wanted a full, unbiased investigation of the case and what led to the sailor's death. At that point, the whole command leadership, especially the department head for the deck department, had to be looked into. The new captain was not going to take any blame for the poor leadership of the former captain.

After an exhaustive couple of weeks of a full investigation, the chiefs who were perpetrating the harassment of the young female sailors were finally identified. Two of them were in the deck department, and one was in operations. The story had already leaked to the inner circles of the squadron, and the commodore had to send his second-in-command to come aboard and evaluate the situation.

The deputy commodore came aboard with a group of JAGs, or judge advocate general staff, a fancy acronym for Navy lawyers. All of a sudden, the initial protection that the chiefs had garnered from their department heads and the former captain, i.e., the refusal to investigate those alleged to have abused their power against poor, non-white female sailors, had evaporated. Everyone from the command master chief all the way to the department heads for deck and operations was implicated. Everyone started to work on saving their own skin.

The commodore gave two weeks for the investigation to come up with findings, and the captain was instructed to deliver the results of the investigation no later than a week thereafter. The chaplain, Dr.

Khalid, and Senior Chief Nicole had already gathered the information they needed. The captain ordered the XO to give the JAGs all the records they needed to complete their investigation.

Multiple enlisted young men and women were initially hesitant to come out and tell the truth about what happened with the dead sailor and those who had been medically discharged. They were afraid of their chiefs, who allegedly threatened them with forced discharge from the Navy and other punishments. However, they were assured that telling the truth and nothing, but the truth would set them free, that they owed it to their dead fellow sailor. In their hearts, those young sailors wanted to cooperate, but forces beyond their control had intimidated them. However, with the new captain, they were given full support and immunity.

The enlisted sailors in the deck department came forward and reported that some chiefs were abusing the younger female sailors, and although some relationships were consensual, it was wrong for a chief to date a twenty-year-old female under his supervision. As per rules in the military, fraternization with the ship's crew was unacceptable; however, it was reported that one chief had been dating one of the young females who were medically discharged. The young lady had told her friends that she really did not want to do it, but the chief was threatening to force her out of the Navy, and since she had confided in him when she first arrived on the ship about how she had no family to return to and that the Navy was going to be her family, he used that against her and took advantage of her vulnerability. She reported to the senior chief that she wanted to be transferred from the deck department, but her abuser refused and said that she was a great worker, and he did not want her to leave the deck. After that, she started to be depressed and had difficulty eating.

The sailors went on to say that the young lady accepted her fate and went along with whatever her abuser wanted, to the point where the abuser took her out to town and told her he was going to buy her gifts. This was his way of appeasing her, but it went beyond that. He wanted her to bring her girlfriends and invite them to a party at his Norfolk home. She then brought four of her best friends with her. The chief had a house on the beach, and he invited three other chiefs, two from the deck department and one from operations. It was a night of drinking and partying. Some of the girls were not even old enough to legally drink.

At the party, it was obvious to all that the deck chief and his young sailor were a couple. However, the chiefs told the girls that they were not to disclose this to anyone, or they would be in deep trouble. The chiefs had so much power over those poor kids. The girls were young and silly, and after a night of drinking, the chiefs did what they had planned. The girls realized that what had happened the night before was wrong and that they needed to report the incident up their chain of command. That was when they were threatened by chiefs and other enlisted leaders. The girls felt cornered and uncared for. The only hope they had was the newly arrived senior supply chief, who, as previously mentioned, wanted to uncover the abuse, but sadly, she was sidelined by the command master chief.

With abusive chiefs and nobody else to run to for help, the young sailors continued to suffer from undiagnosed depression and despondence. By the time the medical department identified the source of the problem and the mental illness caused by the abuse and lack of caring, it was too late, and one sailor had taken her own life. Furthermore, the investigation uncovered after contacting the four sailors who had been medically discharged that they had been forced into unwanted relationships by their department chiefs and the guilt and anger they had suffered had caused their depression and mental anguish.

The report concluded that there were multiple system failures.

First, the chiefs were let loose with impunity, and they did what they wanted with no consideration for the ethical requirements of the US Navy, which discourages the fraternization of high-ranking chiefs and their lower-ranking enlisted members. Second, the chiefs broke the law by having a house party and allowing minors to drink illegal alcohol. Third, after getting the young ladies drunk, they assaulted them without their consent. Fourth, after the complaints were made, the ships' commanding officer and command master chief failed to enforce the Navy rules and did not support those young and vulnerable members under their command. Fifth, command leadership declined to train the crew on sexual harassment prevention.

At the conclusion of the report, the investigation ruled that the deceased sailor had been pushed to the point of suicide because of the abuse of her superior chief and command's ineffectual response to her complaints. This was collaborated by the attending psychiatrist at the Navy clinic at Camp Lomminier, who attested that the symptoms of the four ladies who were under his psychiatric care were consistent with post-traumatic stress disorder, common among physically and sexually abused victims.

The investigators also concluded that it was command's ineptitude and lack of competence to address the complaints of those young ladies, and the lack of leadership by not bringing those responsible to face justice, that caused the loss of life. Command also gave a green light for the warrant officers, who thought they could get away with doing the same thing as they continued to abuse the sailors under their care. This was what happened at the Inter-Continental Hotel in Port Aqaba, Jordan. Those junior officers felt untouchable because they figured if the chiefs could do it without consequences, they could also take advantage of the young and innocent sailors.

What was extremely abhorrent was that when a black, Latino, or Filipino sailor had committed any type of infarction, there was full punishment, including demotion, removal of awards or full-blown expulsion from the service. These negatively impacted those young minority sailor's lives, because, when they got a less-than-honorable discharge, that stayed on their records for life, which affected their employment opportunities beyond the military. They also suffered economic setbacks, as the only skills they had were what the military had taught them. The fact that there was a different set of laws for white sailors was very demoralizing. They looked out for each other; as abusive as the chiefs were to some white female sailors, they never punished them for any wrongdoing.

Dr. Khalid, who had been blind to these facts before his time in the Navy, was very disappointed. His experiences showed him that the only difference between this Navy and America in the 1960s was the integration of races; the application of justice and fairness was still based on one's skin color. It became apparent that if those who were wearing the same uniforms and going to war for defending the Constitution against both foreign and domestic enemies could not be treated equally, then main street America was not going to provide fair and equal justice for all. This fact of life in America was what led to many protests and civil unrest, because there has always been a different application of justice for the different races.

After completion of his sea duty, Dr. Khalid left the Navy and went on to practice medicine in a private setting, while at the same time attending a local teaching hospital. His ideal of America, full equality and justice for all, had been dashed by his years in the Navy; he'd come back still appreciative of the career and education that America had offered him, but less than proud of the treatment of people based not on the content of their character, but the color of their skin.

That bittersweet experience while in uniform was nothing

compared to what Dr. Khalid saw during his tenure at a major hospital when he had firsthand insight into how the COVID-19 pandemic had disproportionately affected the people of color in America. One of the reasons why many African Americans and Hispanics were getting infected and dying from the disease was that they were forced to work. While the white majority had jobs that were mainly white-collar occupations where their companies were able to pay them as they worked from home, the minority members of the American labor force were required to show up to work. They were the so-called "essential workers," the bus drivers, home health workers, nurses' aides, environmental workers, security guards, hospital cleaners, and transportation assistants. Those people could not work from home. They were also less likely to have their own vehicles, so they had to use public transportation, which put them even more at risk of contracting the virus and potentially bringing it back home to their families. Furthermore, as multi-generational families live in the same household among the Hispanics and blacks in America, exacerbated by the downturn in the economy and the increased unemployment, the spread of the virus was made even worse where the younger ones brought the virus back home to their elderly grandparents.

Having awakened to the unfair treatment of minority sailors, Dr. Khalid started to pay more attention to the plight of those underserved members of the community. After the murder of George Floyd in Minnesota, the country experienced a long period of protests in all major cities, from Los Angeles in the west to New York on the East Coast. Young people of all colors and socioeconomic backgrounds marched for the idea of equal justice for blacks in America. Those young people poked their parents in the eye, parents who, even if they were aware of the unequal dispensing of justice and maltreatment of African Americans in the most powerful country in the world, stayed indifferent and silent. Those parents were shamed by their kids; while the young millennials risked their lives by marching in Washington, DC, and other major cities with Black Lives Matter signs over their heads, they reminded older generations of the ancient saying by Dante: "The hottest places in Hell are reserved for those who, in times of moral crisis, maintain their neutrality."

Dr. Khalid was no exception; his teenage kids were beside themselves when they saw their cohorts marching in the streets of Washington in protest of the brutal killing of George Floyd and many other innocent blacks in the streets of America. Of course, Dr. Khalid was more touched when his fourteen-year-old daughter cried and wanted to go and protest and express her feelings. She wanted to take part in this historic moment, to show solidarity with her countrymen. Dr. Khalid was more concerned about the risk of COVID-19 exposure, but in the end, he realized how emotional his kids were and how much they wanted to be apart of this cause; that was bigger than anyone.

He finally relented and decided that he was going to take the kids to Washington to protest. The family started making protesting posters, boards, and pamphlets for the occasion. One of the most interesting ones, which his youngest daughter made, said, "The Color of My Skin Should Not Be a Target on My Back." That poster spoke volumes about the realities in America and how the color of blacks' skin exposed them to unwarranted death in their native home.

The next morning, Dr. Khalid drove the kids to the Metro station, where they took the train to downtown Washington. After thirty-one years of life in America, that was the first public protest that Dr. Khalid took part in. He felt liberated and relieved that he could finally say, and show pictures to prove it, that he'd taken part in a historic civil protest. Dr. Khalid was even happier to see how much his children appreciated that they were apart of this historic moment.

From that moment on, Dr. Khalid was more in touch and aware of the different opinions and feelings he and his children had with respect to being black in America. Their visceral awareness of the racism and maltreatment of blacks in America was much different than that of Dr. Khalid. This was a very common occurrence among the immigrant communities in America, where the political and social opinions of the non-native parents often collided with those of their native children and grandchildren.

So, Dr. Khalid began to pay more attention to the plight of minority employees that he came across in his places of work. If he saw a hospital worker that he suspected of needing help, he was always attentive and deferential to them. This was especially true during the COVID-19 pandemic, when he became keener and more aware of his surroundings.

At the university hospital where he worked part time, Dr. Khalid befriended a gentleman who had been working there for decades. His name was Mr. Albert, and he was a very hard-working family man. Due to insufficient income from the hospital, he started a second job as a security guard with a private company that the hospital had contracted to manage the parking department. He worked at the hospital from 6:30 in the morning till 3:00 pm, only to switch to the parking security until midnight. As a hospital transportation aid, his job was to take patients on the stretcher from one side of the hospital to another. During the normal functioning of the hospital, his duties entailed taking patients to the operating room and back. At the most unfortunate of times, Albert would take a deceased patient from the ward to the hospital morgue. The COVID-19 pandemic meant that Albert was exposed to many patients, both dead and dying of the virus.

So, Dr. Khalid wanted to know how Albert felt about the danger of his occupation. Albert was frank about his feelings; he told the doctor that he was more worried for his wife, Hilda, who was also working at the same hospital as a housekeeping supervisor. He said that housekeepers sometimes didn't get enough cleaning materials and, because of the high rate of infection and hospitalization, the housekeepers were being overwhelmed. Albert also mentioned that they both had elderly parents that they cared for, and every time they needed to visit them, they were extremely worried about the risk of getting them infected.

Albert was so worried about his wife that it didn't register that he might be more at risk, as he was in close contact with infected patients when he transported them, but caring husband that he was, he contemplated asking his wife to quit working there. With two kids in college, however, they could not afford for her to quit her job. Hilda wanted to make sure that her daughters finished college and would do better than their parents. Both she and her husband had made a pact that they would work as hard as possible to ensure that the girls graduated without any loans. The fact that neither one of them had been able to go to college was more fuel to the energy of one day fulfilling that dream for their two girls.

Sabrina was in her second year in college and was studying journalism. She aspired to one day become a cable news anchor. She was the one who kept everyone in the loop about current events, both local and international.

Their older daughter, Lisa, was in law school, so she was more established in financing her education, though she still needed occasional assistance from her parents. Albert told Dr. Khalid that Lisa had recently informed the family that she'd gotten engaged to a young man from California. Chad had gone to college with Lisa; he'd studied communications, while Lisa had majored in political science. He was the one who encouraged Lisa to pursue a law degree. Chad came from a very liberal Jewish family and had been introduced to Lisa during the protests after the killing of Michael Brown.

Chad wrote many articles about police brutality in America and how black men and women in America are mistreated at the hands of the police. He became a Capitol Hill correspondent for a major newspaper. His work in Congress and other governmental agencies of both the Executive and Legislative Branches had given him firsthand inside information through leaks and networking. Therefore, Chad was always on the cusp of what was happening in the most powerful halls of the most powerful town.

To garner full support from his skeptical but, hopefully, future in-laws, and especially Lisa's father, Chad was always the one to share the most secretive leaks from Capitol Hill with the old man. This connection between Chad and Albert became a two-way beneficial relationship, which Lisa was very grateful for. While both parents were supportive of her decisions in general, they did not hide the fact that Lisa and Chad were not going to face an easy union in today's racially charged America. They blessed the decision nonetheless.

Albert lamented how the government was not helping people like him, who were unable to stay home, while those with huge salaries were given extra money and large businesses were able to apply for huge loans. He expressed the feeling of despair that those already set in life were getting more than their fair share. Albert was a very smart man; although he never went to college, he had a greater sense than many educated people. As Mark Twain put it, "Don't let schooling interfere with your education." It seemed Albert did not need a degree to be the extremely intelligent and well-read man he appeared to be.

He pointed out to Dr. Khalid, who also shared with him a lot of his life experiences, that the America that did not give a hoot about the well-being of it's African American citizens was becoming a menace to them ever since the election of Donald Trump. The fact that so many minorities were dying in big cities like New York and Washington, DC, and the federal government was not even discussing ways to mitigate the pandemic was a clear signal to Albert that the Trump administration cared more about campaigning than caring for its citizens. As Albert continued sharing his worries with Dr. Khalid, he pointed out how the White House, rather than showing real leadership and grit, and perhaps using the pandemic to unite the divided country, they continued to sow the seeds of division. The America that used to rally together in times of war and national distress was divided into two camps: those who followed the public health measures of wearing masks and practicing self-distancing and those who believed that the virus was a hoax, as the president told them.

At that moment, Dr. Khalid realized that Albert would be a great addition to the forum and his intellect and life experience could be a great asset to the group. As he was departing for home, he shared with Albert that there was a discussion group about the current situation and the plight of blacks in America and how to come up with a solution to the long-lasting maltreatment of blacks at the hands of the police. Dr. Khalid explained to Albert that the group had been created to instill awareness and to educate the African American youth as well as anyone interested in finding a solution to the problem. Dr. Khalid explained the groups' main objective of teaching people of African heritage how they could get in touch with their motherland: through education, volunteerism, tourism, or business investment.

Albert was delighted to join the group, and the two agreed to see each other at the next meeting. Albert asked if his family could join to hear about the group as well. Dr. Khalid replied, "The more, the merrier."

As soon as Albert went in to work his second job at the security office, an urgent call came from his wife. She told him that she was not herself; she mentioned a scratchy throat and intermittent cough. She suggested that she was going to get tested as soon as possible. He told her he was on his way to meet her at the hospital. Hilda got tested, as those with possible exposure and symptoms were given priority. Her rapid COVID-19 test returned positive, and she was ordered to self-isolate for fourteen days. Albert was devastated; although he was negative, it was bad enough that his wife was getting sick and his worst worries had come true. The next big worry for both Albert and Hilda was to see if their senior parents had been infected, as they have visited them over the weekend. Albert's parents lived about twenty minutes away, so he did not want to risk visiting. Instead, he arranged for their home health nurse to arrange a test out of an abundance of caution. Hilda's mom lived by herself; she was also told to get tested. The results for Albert's parents were negative, but Hilda's mom was positive, and she was ordered to self-isolate. The sad part was that a sickly, elderly lady had to be isolated from others.

That week, the number of cases in the country skyrocketed, with a high rate of death among minorities. Hilda isolated herself in the basement of the house; unfortunately, her symptoms continued to worsen, with severe coughs, head and body aches, and extremely high fever. The family debated whether to take her to the hospital or keep her at home as long as breathing was not a problem. The reluctance to consider taking Hilda to the hospital had to do with a rumor that the rate of death among the hospitalized COVID-19 patients was very high and the lack of confidence that, as a black patient, she would get the care she was going to need there. This made Albert very sad about the fact that the trust of health care providers was even in doubt in America, that a citizen of this country could not trust the care of his or her hospitals. Tears came to his eyes as he despondently shook his head at the fact that African Americans could not run to a police officer for security, nor to a physician for health care. He said to himself, "What a messed-up place to be in."

He consulted with his daughters, and the family decided that Hilda would stay home as long as her breathing was normal. With her oximeter on her index finger, Albert and the girls continued to monitor her and made sure her oxygen level was at ninety-five percent.

Luckily, Hilda recovered and returned to her normal activities.

A couple of weeks after Hilda was cleared of the viral infection, her mom's condition took a turn for the worse. She started having difficulty breathing. After consultation with her doctor, the family was forced to take the seventy-nine-year-old to the local hospital. Initially, the hospital was able to stabilize her without having to move her to the critical care unit; unfortunately, her condition deteriorated, and after less than a week at the hospital, Hilda's mom had to be intubated. With age and other underlying conditions, including a history of heart disease and diabetes, Hilda lost her mom to COVID-19.

It was a devastating loss for Hilda; an only child, she was very close to her mom. Having grown up without siblings, Hilda's mom was her sister and best friend. Hilda went through a long bout of depression and despair due to the death of her mom, but life had to go on, and for her family's sake, she picked up the pieces and lived for the living.

A few months after the passing of Hilda's mom, Chad called Albert and told him that he was about to break a huge story in the newspaper. He wanted Albert to be the first to know before it was published. Chad had already made sure that he'd told Lisa the idea first, and she had given him the green light. This was a huge leak from the powers that be. As disorganized and incompetent as the Trump administration was, there were always leaks and a continuous bleeding of dirty laundry by either silent whistleblowers or well-intentioned people who found themselves more effective when screaming from within.

Chad did not want the news to be shared on the phone, as he did not want any eavesdroppers to highjack the story before it was published, but he also wanted to gain more favor from Albert by impressing him with a face-to-face meeting; he really wanted Lisa's hand, so anything to butter up her father was going to help the cause. Albert was very excited and could hardly wait.

The two met at a local coffee shop, and Chad started his meeting with a precautionary note that what he was about to tell Albert was going to cause him a lot of pain, especially with Hilda just coming back to being normal after the infection and the loss of her mom. He also told him that the story was not yet published, so Albert had to keep it to himself till then. This was the kind of story that won Washington journalists huge professional rewards.

Chad told Albert that one of his most reliable sources leaked to him, on the condition of anonymity, that the White House policy regarding COVID-19 and how it was affecting blacks and other minorities was discussed in great detail. The idea of giving more assistance to those majority-black cities where both the death and the infection rates were high was on the agenda. The source further described that leadership refused to give any assistance to those minority communities because they did not support the president during the last election and were less likely to vote for the Republican ticket this time around. The source added that since those cities were run by Democrats, their incompetence was the source of the high death rate. The source pointed out that some of those who were against helping their fellow American citizens were arguing that Republican-run cities and states were functioning better and that was why they did not report any deaths or infections.

When some public health officials in the meeting objected to the abhorrent idea of letting some of their fellow Americans to suffer this way, they were rebuffed by some of the anti-immigration hawks, who argued that those cities were breaking American immigration law as defined by the president's executive order in that they willingly harbored illegal immigrants as sanctuary cities.

Chad continued, describing how his source was amazed by the action of those hardliners who were willingly putting American lives at risk by knowingly withholding funds to keep people alive and the pandemic under control.

Albert was shocked but not surprised. This story surely proved what he had been thinking that those who were in the position of power to help the needy withheld from their fellow Americans what could have saved their lives. To Albert, it became unclear which evil was worse: the police, who continued killing blacks in America for the simplest crimes, or the elected officials who knowingly refused to help those dying from the pandemic that was killing people by the thousands each day. To Albert, who had lost a family member to the disease as well as countless coworkers and family friends, it was personal. He wondered if there was an intentional aim to let people of color die.

He asked himself what had always made a white police officer want to shoot with the intention of killing black men and women in America. They could arrest them without shedding any blood; they had the guns. And if they were so bloodthirsty as to shed black people's blood, why couldn't they incapacitate them? Why not shoot them in the lower extremities so their coward selves could be assured that the suspect wouldn't run away or beat the hell out of them, like they always feared?

# 5

# NIKKI

"I've learned that people will forget what you said, people will forget what you did, but people will never forget how you made them feel." **Maya Angelou**

Nikki, the nurse practitioner, had her own experience as a black woman in America. She was born in Indianapolis, Indiana, to a middle-class African American community in the 1960s. She studied social work at Indiana University for her first degree. Her family belonged to the prominent and thriving community of Indiana Avenue, a historic landmark for successful business areas in the Midwest for blacks from the early 1900s to the 1950s. As one of her graduation requirements, Nikki did a research paper on the causes of the decline of Indiana Avenue and the Black Wall Street of that era.

In her well-presented academic paper, Nikki discussed how Indianapolis had a very glamorous black history, with thriving businesses and cultural centers. Indiana Avenue had jazz and blues entertainment centers, where notables like Duke Ellington, Cab Calloway, and Ella Fitzgerald were known to perform. As locals, the Hampton Sisters and West Montgomery were also well known there. The success of black culture and music was paralleled by that of business icons like Madam C.J. Walker's thriving banking and hair care products company. The area had over four hundred acres of businesses, such as black-owned and employed banks, stores, music clubs, churches, theatres, barbershops, doctor's offices, and funeral homes. The black people of Indianapolis did not need to leave their neighborhood for groceries or self-grooming needs. Blacks all over America came to Indianapolis to see what business success looked like so they could go back to their cities and replicate the brand. Whether it was entrepreneurship, banking, commerce, or music, Indiana Avenue was the Mecca of black pride.

According to Nikki's paper, this success occurred not because of civil rights or equal justice. As a matter of fact, one of the last lynching in America occurred in Marion, Indiana. Also, the KKK had over 250,000 of its members in the state. Those who were members of the Klan included the Indiana governor at the time and the mayor of Indianapolis, but those bigots left Indiana Avenue alone. Other than the successful businesses owned by blacks, there were also the European immigrants, but the area was known to have malaria, and the white supremacists did not want to get mixed up with the malaria-carrying blacks of Indiana Avenue.

Because of all the successful businesses owned by blacks, the black population of the city grew substantially as many non-Indiana residents moved from other states, especially the South, where things were horrible for blacks. The turning point in the success of the blacks in Indianapolis was marked by the relocation of Madam Walker's business headquarters to Indiana Avenue. She increased the labor force and employment among the black residents of Indianapolis tremendously. She tapped the leadership of the black community to increase the visibility of the black people's ability to own businesses and hire among their own. Madam Walker also assisted black neighborhoods civically and socially; she raised funds to build the black branch of the YMCA in the city. She developed the Walker Building, which had become her business management center; it was later named the Walker Theatre. It was said that by the time she died in 1919, Madam C.J. Walker was the wealthiest self-made woman in America. Her contribution to black success through loans for small businesses, homeowners' mortgages, and other means of financing was instrumental in the success of blacks in Indianapolis.

But, as Nikki's parents related to her, as they were getting ready to raise their family in the middle of the 1950s, the decline of the black businesses started. This was due to discriminatory practices against black-owned businesses. There were redlining practices, whereby white-owned banks would deny black business owners loans to improve or expand their businesses. Homeowners who were not white, like Nikki's parents, were denied home improvement loans, and those who wanted to own new homes could not purchase them. As the most tangible way to pass on wealth among generations is homeownership, those who were lucky enough to own homes could not afford the upkeep of those properties. That led to the dilapidation of those properties to the point of disrepair.

It seemed as though the destruction of black success on Indianapolis's Indiana Avenue was by design. As Nikki put it, as soon as those properties and businesses, including her parents', went belly up, the city decided that the neighborhood needed to be demolished and rebuilt. The Indiana University had its eye on the black neighborhood for its planned expansion, and as soon as the area was declared blighted by the city, the land was allocated for the university's medical center. Those residents who resisted moving and were able to repair their properties were forced out through eminent domain. Nikki's parents lost their home that way and were forced to relocate elsewhere in the city. Fortunately, her parents could afford to move the family to a decent neighborhood; however, the majority of blacks who were forced from their neighborhood, where they had lived for generations, found themselves destitute. Some were housed in unsafe, unsanitary, and crowded slums, where many children died in fires and electrical accidents. Nikki pointed out that the unsafe conditions of some living quarters contributed to the death of over twenty children in less than twelve months after the forced move.

Nikki was able to attend good schools; her father was a funeral director and moved the business to a more central location. One of the good things about being a funeral director was that people were sentenced to die, and her father had a great clientele, not only among the blacks in the city, but also the European immigrants, who, at the time, had not assimilated into mainstream white America. So, her family was able to educate Nikki and her brothers.

After graduating from high school, Nikki got a full scholarship from Indiana University. She really wanted to go to Howard and experience the historically black university, but her father told her that Indiana University had taken her inheritance when they'd forced them out of her childhood home; therefore, she should not pass up the opportunity to get back at them and take advantage of the free four-year education. She could not resist the temptation for vengeance, so she went to Indiana University.

Her father's stories and the history she had read about the wrong that had been done to the black community of Indianapolis led her to study the circumstances that had surrounded the black lives of the city. One of the bad memories still on her mind was the police killing of her stepbrother, Anthony, who had been attending college in Fort Wayne. He was wrongly identified as a burglar when he got lost at night while driving home from Ohio. As he pulled over in a neighborhood that was all white to ask for directions, the neighbors called the police to report a burglary in progress. The argument between Anthony and the police led to his shooting and death. The investigation that followed found that the police had been within their rights to shoot him, and no action was taken against the officers involved.

While studying at Indiana University, Nikki did an internship at the university hospital as a resident social worker and patient advocate. This training gave her firsthand experience and knowledge about the health care disparities among the races in the city. Way before the term "implied racism" came to the forefront, she saw how black patients at the main hospital and clinics, which were state-sponsored and financed through Medicaid, were treated. Nikki reported how African American patients who complained about pain were never taken seriously and were treated as though they were seeking narcotics just to get high, while white patients were catered to like they were on vacation. It was like night and day how the nurses, and even some doctors, discriminated against those poor patients.

One afternoon, Nikki was at the hospital and rotating through the OB/GYN department when a heavily pregnant African American female about twenty-five years old was brought in from the emergency room. She was in extreme distress, and the attending doctor asked her how many months into her pregnancy she was. The patient responded that she was in her late sixth month or early seventh month.

Nikki, who was assisting as the social worker, heard the doctor say, "These people don't even know when they get pregnant." The white physician was more worried about whether the patient had gotten the stage of her pregnancy right than her condition and how to be empathetic to a sick patient. He knew that what he'd said was not called for, but as Nikki had witnessed in multiple situations, this was the reality of how black patients were treated by white health care providers.

Nikki was able to look up the patient's information on the hospital's computer system, as the patient had been there before for prenatal care. The doctor did not even try to gather the patient's information. To be exact, the patient was seven months pregnant, and she complained about severe headaches, nausea, and blurry vision. The doctor told her that she just needed to take some Tylenol for the headache and rest at home.

The patient reported to the nurse that this was not her first pregnancy and that she had never felt this way with her previous two pregnancies. She requested that the physician do a more thorough assessment. Both Nikki and the nurse went back to the doctor's office to relay the message that the patient was not satisfied with his answer and needed more assessment. He replied to the nurse that she would be fine, to just let her take Tylenol and rest up. When the nurse told him that the patient had reported that she'd never felt this way with her previous pregnancies, the doctor replied sarcastically that she must have started having kids when she was a teenager. Nikki could not handle this one and told the physician that what was really important was that the patient got the care she needed; that it was nobody's business how early she started to have kids.

The doctor got very upset and told Nikki that he was the doctor and, if she needed to do that type of a job, she needed to go back to school and put in years and years of hard work and study. He told them that the patient needed to follow his instructions and go home to rest. Nikki and the nurse did not have the authority to change his mind; as he said, he was the doctor, and that was it. The patient was given the headache medicine and sent home.

Nikki and the nurse became really good friends. The nurse, who had over ten years of OB/GYN experience at many hospitals, told

Nikki that she suspected that the young lady might have a condition called pre-eclampsia, which could be very deadly if misdiagnosed. The nurse explained that the young lady had the hallmarks of the condition, including headaches, blurred vision, swollen extremities, and nausea. The nurse was an immigrant from the Philippines; she had seen many cases of complicated pregnancies, and she knew that the patient had not been given the proper assessment, but only doctors were legally allowed to diagnose, and there was nothing she could do to sway his decision to send the patient home.

That was when Nikki decided that she was going to continue her studies to become either a physician or a nurse. She had no doubt that if that physician had been black, he would not have disregarded that patient or mistreated her like that white doctor did. After a long day at the hospital, she went home wondering how many pregnant black women were sent home without proper treatment.

Nikki was doing her hospital internship at a different location when she received a phone call from the nurse she had worked with just two days before at the hospital. The nurse told her the most heart-wrenching and distressing news, and she cried while trying to explain what had happened.

The young black female who was pregnant came back to the hospital a few days after Nikki had been there. The patient was much worse, and her headaches were not alleviated by the medicine the doctor suggested. She was vomiting and unable to focus. She was immediately taken for evaluation, and the attending physician diagnosed her with late-stage preeclampsia. The doctor ordered an immediate C-section after informing the patient's family that if they did not deliver the baby immediately, they could both die. The consent was signed, and the patient was rolled into the operating room without delay. The baby was delivered but was stillborn. The mother suffered a major stroke during the C-section due to the previously undiagnosed extreme hypertension; unfortunately, she also passed away.

Nikki was devastated. She felt that if only the patient had been properly treated the first time and her symptoms addressed instead of judging her, the outcome could have been different. Although she knew that she was not the doctor and her voice had been irrelevant at the time, she still felt that she'd failed in her duty to advocate for the patient. Both Nikki and the nurse were saddened by what had happened.

At the university, Nikki had been a very loud voice for advancing the rights of minority patients and she had always tried to speak out against the unfair treatment of those who were underserved. She'd seen firsthand how hospitals and health care professionals treat patients differently based on their race and ability to pay for the services. It was unbelievable that some providers always assumed that if a patient was black, they must be using some type of government-subsidized insurance plan, such as Medicaid. Minority patients were always asked, "Do you have your Medicaid card?" or told, "Have your Medicaid card ready when you get in the waiting line." The white patients, who, per capita, used Medicaid more than any other group, were never asked such a question. It was a biased attitude about non-white patients: they must be the poor and destitute.

Nikki graduated with a Bachelor of Science in Social Work. Before her last year there, she had already applied and been accepted to a combined BS/MS program in nursing with the intention of becoming a nurse practitioner. Her goal was to make a change in the health care disparities among the black community, to highlight the mistreatment of black patients by health care providers. She wanted to wage a new civil rights movement in the delivery of health care in America. Her experience in the area of social work and concentration in health care delivery systems had prepared her for her crusade against the unjust discrimination of patients of color.

While she studied for her nursing degrees, she suggested to the nursing faculty that it was very important that incoming medical students be trained in how to be empathetic towards patients of color and different socio-economic status so that when they become licensed physicians, they provided the best care to all patients, regardless of race or ability to afford the proper care that everyone deserves to have. The faculty members were extremely impressed with her experience and interest in the area of health care disparities, and the nursing school invited her to prepare a lecture series on the subject so that nurses could benefit from her insights. The nursing school made Nikki an adjunct instructor to teach first-year nursing and medical Students the ethics of health care. This course was very helpful for Nikki, too, as she learned so much about clinical care and how to maximize patient care outcomes through cultural awareness and direct communication. She instilled in these future doctors and nurses the importance of listening to patients before judging them.

After the successful completion of her RN and nurse practitioner training, Nikki was hired by one of the most prominent hospitals on the East Coast. She had also written multiple articles on the subject of access to health care among underserved communities in the United States, and her insights and experience as a social worker and practicing nurse contributed to the excellent care provided by the agencies of which she was a part.

As a child growing up in Indianapolis, Nikki was no stranger to racial inequality, discrimination, and bias. Even as she went on a successful journey as a student and educator, she continued to pay close attention to how America was stuck in its past. Over the years, she came face to face with racism in America. As an educated black woman who was never afraid to speak up when she saw unfair treatment, she was viewed by many as an unreasonable and angry woman, but she wasn't prepared to face what happened to her nephew, a promising, smart eighteen-year-old boy named Jamal who was on his high school football team and was accepted to one of the Ivy League universities.

Nikki's older brother, Michael, was a cardiologist at a local hospital. He had a family of his own, with two girls already in college and the youngest, Jamal, still at home. His wife, Lydia, was a former respiratory therapist he had met during his hospital residency in Cleveland, Ohio.

One day, like any teenager wanting to drive their parents' expensive car, the young man asked his father if he could run to his friend's house. His father allowed him to drive his Mercedes Benz S500. Jamal was extremely delighted to show off his father's nice car. The neighborhood where his friend lived was only eight miles away. On his way back home, he was pulled over by a local police officer. Jamal knew what to do; his father had trained him to be polite and respectful to anyone in authority, especially police officers. Michael had told all his children that it behooved any black person stopped by the police to keep their cool. "Confronting trigger-happy cops will only put you in more danger," he told them. He always stressed that it was better to swallow your pride than cease swallowing altogether after getting shot by an uneducated police officer. Even if the officer were found guilty, nothing would bring a dead black person back.

So, the young man knew what to do. He kept his hands visible and on the wheel. He already had his wallet with his driver's license on the dashboard, so it was ready to show the officer. However, he recorded on his phone everything the officer said. The cop told him in a threatening voice, "Get out of the car quickly and keep your hands up!" The cop was holding his right hand on his hip, ready with the pistol. His loud and aggressive voice made the teenager extremely nervous, but the young man kept his cool. The officer told him to get his driver's license out, so, he did. He told the boy to hold his hands up and place his body against the car. All the while, the boy did what was told without complaint.

DR. KASEY Y. FARAH

The officer did a complete search of Jamal's pockets. Although Jamal was aware of his father's advice to follow the officer's instructions, he knew that searching someone without a warrant is illegal, so he told the officer that. This really struck a nerve with the officer, who became even more agitated, and he radioed for backup from the station.

The officer continued interrogating the teenager, asking him where he'd stolen the car from. Perplexed by the question, Jamal answered that he did not steal any car and that it was his father's. With a smirk on his face, the officer again asked the boy where he'd stolen the car. At that point, the boy was holding his hands against the car, petrified that the officer, whose hand never left his gun, might suddenly shoot him. Any movement by the boy could result in the officer discharging his weapon and killing him.

Imagine a young, scared black boy being harassed by a white police officer with a gun, a young black boy who had seen so many police executions of innocent black men at the hands of white police officers. Many of these men, after being wrongly accused of crimes they did not commit, ran for their lives, only to be shot in the back by the police. Luckily, Jamal kept his cool and did as the policeman asked.

After a few minutes, another police car with its lights on pulled up. That police officer started looking through the Mercedes to check for drugs or guns. Nothing was found. The new officer then started the interrogation of the teenager all over again. Jamal continued to tell the truth, that the car was his father's.

The first officer asked Jamal if he lived in a certain neighborhood. That area was known to be a housing project, and the officer was making a racist assumption that, as a black kid, he must live on the bad side of town and for him to be in this neighborhood was akin to trespassing. Jamal told him that he did not live there, and they could check his driver's license as to where his address was. The officer asked him what his father did. Jamal told him that his father worked at the city hospital, to which the officer commented that his father must be a watchman there. The eighteen-year-old did not know what a watchman was. He only knew the euphemized term "security guard," and since his generation was taught to be polite, the high school watchmen were not allowed to be called watchmen but security guards.

Jamal told the officer that his father was not a watchman but a cardiologist. The dumb officer then thought about checking the address to make sure the boy was telling the truth. The address on the driver's license matched that of the owner of the car, who happened to be the father of the teenager. Jamal was terrified and did not want to drive the car home. He told the officers that he wanted to make a phone call to his family and he was not feeling well. The police did not want to confront the father, as they realized that they had wronged the boy by assuming that he'd stolen the car. Everything was recorded on Jamal's phone, even if the police camera was off. Jamal insisted on getting his parents to come, so the police had no choice but to allow him to call his parents.

His parents were only five minutes away, so they came without delay. They were both worried that something bad had happened. Jamal's father introduced himself to the officers and asked if Jamal was all right. Jamal told his father that the police had stopped him because they'd thought he had stolen the car. The officer who initially stopped Jamal tried to defend himself, saying that Jamal had been swerving across lanes and he wanted to make sure he was not under the influence. Jamal told his father everything the officers had said about where he lived in the city and that the car was stolen since he could not afford to drive such an expensive one.

Jamal's mother, a white lady, was beside herself, screaming and yelling at the officers. His father, however, kept his cool. He kindly asked the officers to give him their business cards. He told them that he was a well-known cardiologist at the local hospital and wanted to send a compliment to the chief as to how well they'd handled the situation. Jamal could not believe how cool his father was being, but he knew his father was up to something. The officers could not deny the doctor their business cards, although it was written all over their faces that the doc was going to report a complaint.

Jamal's father consulted his attorney to explore if there might be a viable case against the officers for harassing his son and subjugating him to that type of humiliation. He even showed the attorney the recording. The attorney told the family that as long as their son was safe, they should be glad, that trying to go after the police was a futile exercise, as they could claim that the teenager had been violating traffic rules and this and that. The family was very upset about how their son had been mistreated and verbally abused and how this was a classic case of racial profiling.

Jamal was negatively affected by that horrible encounter with the police, and for months, he refused to drive. The family had to seek counseling for their son because of the extreme depression that resulted from his bad experience.

With all the bad personal experiences Nikki had had with racism in America and other stories she'd heard from friends and colleagues, the one that left her with an indelible mark and led her to question the viability of raising a family in America was what had happened to Jamal at the hands of the police. She kept thinking about how the encounter had almost turned tragic. All it would have taken was for Jamal to run from the police—and he would have been right to do so—and they would have shot him down.

From that point on, Nikki started to explore the idea of emigrating from America and settle in Africa. There, she could live a life of dignity and contribute to the development of the motherland. Nikki had friends there with whom she had gone to college and nursing school.

Although she'd lost contact with some of her friends after decades of being apart, she had cultivated her relationships with her African friends. They exchanged birthday and Christmas cards and all kinds of occasional greetings. Her friends even joked about Nikki moving to Africa or retiring there. At the time, the idea was a bit too farfetched; after all, Nikki had parents, siblings, and other relatives in America, and leaving all that behind was not easy. The odds of picking up and moving across the Atlantic were next to nothing. But as she grew older and her parents passed, and with the extreme social changes in America that were not for the better, the idea of leaving her country became more plausible.

She'd always had a heightened interest in Africa, and out of curiosity, she had gone to Africa for visits. The first time, she'd taken part in an African American pilgrimage that encouraged the diaspora to get acquainted with the continent just in case it became necessary for African Americans to consider leaving the New World. Those pilgrims believed that America was never going to embrace blacks. They were of the opinion that after slavery, the white majority was forced to integrate blacks because the law of the land forced them to do so. Therefore, it behooved black Americans to have options, so they created this group that invited African American intellectuals and professionals to go back and visit West Africa, the land of their ancestors, and see what could have been as well as what could be.

After her first visit, Nikki realized that she belonged there; it felt like a religious awakening for her. Being on the African shore of the Atlantic Ocean was like nothing she had ever felt before. Her interest in the West African countries such as Ghana, Senegal, and The Gambia grew every time she went back there. She noticed how stress-free life was for her professional friends there. She made a point to bring up the idea to her family and friends in the US.

The more Nikki thought about the idea of moving to Africa, the more her contemplative idea became more concrete and made complete sense to her. However, she did not just trust her instinct; as a trained nurse and social worker, she wanted to have an educated decision. She did her due diligence to understand the pros and cons of moving to Africa. She did not want to share this with her family until she had answers to every possible question they were going to bring up. After all, leaving her kin and kith behind was not going to be easy.

Nikki started to research African Americans who had moved to Africa to live and how their experiences varied. She went from as far back as W.E.B. Dubois to the present-day diaspora movement to Africa. She evaluated the differing opinions of the many African American and Caribbean activists who had promoted and debated the feasibility of blacks returning to Africa. She went online to understand the history of African American repatriation to the motherland. She also explored the issue on YouTube.

She was extremely surprised that so many professionals had already moved and set up new lives in West Africa. Nikki was dumbfounded that doctors, lawyers, investment bankers, university professors, and business owners had all moved there. She was particularly intrigued by the story of a middle-aged former dentist by the name of Joseph Nightingale, who moved to Ghana twenty years back.

As he described his decision to leave America to Nikki, he said he'd had nothing but trouble in America. He went on to say that every time he thought things were going to get better for blacks in America, he was sorely disappointed. In high school, he'd thought that if he excelled and received great grades, he would be able to go to college and become educated; he'd thought he would be judged by his abilities and achievements. In college, he faced bias and indirect discrimination, so he pursued a doctorate to be among the most well-educated elites, hoping that would grant him the respect and equal treatment that any human being was owed.

After becoming the first in his family to finish college, he went on to dental school. His family was ecstatic to have a doctor in the family. Dr. Nightingale told Nikki that while many of his white dental school friends got loans from their local banks to open brand-new dental practices—and some of them received a turnkey from their dentist fathers--he was unable to get any bank to loan him funds to start a practice of his own. He even tried the Small Business Administration but was denied at every turn.

As the first in his family to attend college, he had no wealth to show for collateral, and many white-owned banks did not want to lend money to an inexperienced black doctor. So, he said he was forced to work for one of his rich white friends whose father had transferred his dental practice to upon graduation.

Dr. Nightingale continued his story by saying that as he was traveling home one night from a long day of work, he was pulled over by a local police officer in Knoxville, Tennessee. He was only traveling five miles over the speed limit, but the officer pulled his gun on him and was ready to fire.

Dr. Nightingale said he made sure to stay calm as the officer held the gun against his jugular vein, his index finger on the trigger. As the police officer was about to shoot, a dispatcher call came to him. The police officer told the dispatcher that a drug dealer thug was resisting arrest and he needed a backup. The caller made the order to start searching the back trunk, so the officer ordered Dr. Nightingale to open the trunk.

Knowing his legal rights, if he had any at that moment, Dr. Nightingale was aware that a search without a warrant was not lawful. But knowing how violent the officer was being towards him and what aggravating this trigger-happy coward would lead to, he obliged and opened the trunk. In the trunk was a briefcase with the University of

Tennessee Dental School logo on it. The moment the officer saw that briefcase, he came around and asked Dr. Nightingale if he was a doctor, and Dr. Nightingale responded that he was. The officer disengaged his pistol and placed it back in its holster. Then he sent a message to his incoming backup officers to abort the mission and gave Dr. Nightingale a halfhearted apology and a ticket for driving five miles over the speed limit.

Dr. Nightingale shared with Nikki that he sat in his car for a long time, unable to drive or do anything due to rage and anger. It frustrated and humiliated him that, as a man close to his thirties, he could not stand up to such abuse and mistreatment in his own country. It reminded him of stories he'd read about Apartheid South Africa and how the police of that era used to abuse black citizens. He wondered why the officer changed his demeanor after seeing the dental school logo.

Dr. Nightingale spoke with some lawyer friends, who told him that there was an unwritten rule among white police officers in some jurisdictions that they should stay away from black doctors and lawyers. The idea was that educated and well-paid blacks could sue and get back at the police. Ironically, when he inquired about pressing charges against the police officer for violating his civil rights, the lawyer told him it would go nowhere and could cause more trouble for him with the police.

Dr. Nightingale told Nikki that this was the last straw for him, and he decided to leave America. When she asked him about his life in Accra, he told her that he'd never felt so liberated in his entire life. He told her that home is where one is happy, appreciated, respected, and valued.

He described how his fellow African brothers and sisters in Ghana had welcomed him like a family. He told Nikki that if he could turn back time, he would have left that place much earlier. He said that the twenty years he had lived in Ghana were the most productive years in his life. He'd built a flourishing practice in Accra. He'd gotten married and started a family where he was not worried about his boys being killed with impunity by the American police. He did not miss the stress of being black in America. He told Nikki that he owed nothing to any bank and he'd paid off everything he owns. He said he felt that being part of the community and the culture of treating people with equal respect was rooted in African customs and tradition, and the sense of feeling valued and respected no matter one's color, creed, or religion made any visitor to the continent fall in love with it. Dr. Nightingale further shared with Nikki that many other Americans who had left for Africa had only great things to say about it. With utmost willingness, he offered to assist anyone wanting to move to the enlightened continent where the past and future of the world meet.

As one of the cross-sectional and multi-generational African American immigrants in West Africa, Nikki also interacted with younger female professionals who had made their truest home there. She met a young lady from New York City who, after years in corporate finance in the world's largest financial district, had found herself disillusioned with the unfairness of life in America. Her name was Justice. Ironically, Justice had to leave America for Africa in search of true justice. After she graduated from an Ivy League college with a double major in corporate finance and marketing and a master's in banking, Justice was offered a mid-level managerial position at one of the largest international banks in New York. She was doing well financially, but as she continued progressing in her position, she became one of the most productive members in her department. She said that she expected her performance to not only be appreciated but also rewarded with promotions and more responsibility. She was not begging it; she felt she deserved to be acknowledged for her success. But the company continued to pass her over.

Justice told Nikki that the only way she could explain why the leadership of the firm did not pay attention to her concerns was that they actually believed that she had already done well enough to be where she was. They wondered what the fuss was all about. To them, a black girl from the South who'd gotten a job on Wall Street was beyond belief. That was one reason why Justice decided she needed to re-evaluate her future there.

Another reason she left America, Justice explained, was that as an educated and successful black female in America, it was extremely difficult to find a suitable future husband as hard-working and successful as her. The reasons for this were many. She pointed out that most African American men were either imprisoned or had some type of criminal history. Due to the unfairness of the justice system, those who broke the law were forever tainted and unable to become gainfully employed even after they did their time. Other potentially suitable mates, because of systemic racism or family problems that had their roots in implicit discrimination, were never able to continue their higher education, and without a college degree, no black man in America has a chance of finding a good job. Justice pointed out that due to the multiple social problems faced by black families in America, many young men did not pursue or value education, and that had created a very imbalanced male-to-female ratio on college campuses.

In a nutshell, for a successful black female, the odds of finding a halfway decent mate of the opposite gender was like looking for a needle in a haystack. So, when Justice saw an opportunity to join an international firm with offices in Accra, where she was given the opportunity to lead an entire department, she said it was time to research the place. She did her research about relocating to Ghana and found out that it was the most frequent destination for young black Americans who wanted to move to Africa. She connected with those who had been there for several years and discovered that many had married native Ghanaians and were happily residing in the capital.

Justice shared with Nikki that when she asked her informants about what was different in Ghana, their response was that everything; that all the differences from America were positive: no discrimination, no hate for anyone based on color or creed, less expensive way of life, and many ladies were ecstatic to have found their lifelong loves there.

Justice said that with the financial package and promotion she had been offered, plus all the other advantages shared by those who had arrived there before her, she had been totally sold on the idea of packing up and leaving for Africa. She further shared that although she had been mentally prepared for some culture shock, she had been absolutely blown away by how wrong she was. She found the people to be extremely polite and welcoming. She loved her place of work and was given many amenities and assistance in her transition there. She pointed out that the stress of living she'd experienced in America was suddenly gone. Her bosses were so great, and the employees she supervised were unbelievably helpful.

Justice reported that after working there for less than a year, she met her husband at a financial conference in Abuja, Nigeria. He was representing another bank in Ghana. Julius was executive vice president of a bank in Accra. After they met in Nigeria, they realized that they were representing two rival banks, so they exchanged contact information and decided to reconnect back in Accra.

A few weeks after their initial meeting, Justice received a phone call from Julius. Her secretary, who knew Julius through the department of banking relations, was astonished that someone of that caliber was calling her boss. She rushed to Justice's office and said, "Mr. Julius, the VP of Commercial Bank, is on the phone for you, madam." Justice did not get the urgency with which her secretary was trying to relay the message, so she told her that she would call him back and her secretary should take a message. With extreme reluctance, the secretary closed the door and took down the message, telling Julius that Madam Justice was very busy and was very sorry about not taking the call at that moment but would call back as soon as humanly possible.

Justice felt the behavior of her secretary was kind of weird, and when she heard how apologetic her secretary was about the call, she came out of her office and asked her what the issue was. Her secretary told her that Julius was a very high-ranking official in banking circles and she felt that his call should have been answered. Justice told her that she'd met him in Nigeria and she was going to return the call. The secretary was used to having other office aides calling on behalf of their bosses to arrange meetings and business matters; she'd never had a call from a president of a bank.

So, the next day Justice returned the call. As she had expected, the call was not related to a business matter; Julius wanted to have a social meeting with her. He told her that he had been thinking about her ever since they had met at the conference in Abuja and had been struggling to decide how best to reach out. He invited her to a casual dinner meeting whenever she was available. Justice accepted the invitation. The two met for a lavish dinner, followed by a movie.

The dating continued for months, and the two were happy in each other's company. Julius had an oceanside villa where he went on weekends to relax. Justice and some of her friends started to join him for group barbecues and social networking. Justice got to know Julius very well. Soft-spoken and on the religious side, he was very calm and collected. He was one of the top financial gurus in the country and often traveled around the world for banking and financial conferences. He told Justice that he could not count how many times he had traveled to the States for World Bank conferences and many other regional meetings. Julius was five years her senior; with more experience and an easygoing manner, he grounded Justice and calmed her feisty American way of looking at things. To her credit, Justice realized that her new companion's experience and diplomacy were traits that she could benefit from. It appeared that Julius had all the characteristics that Justice was searching for in a future husband: economic stability, kindness, mutual love, and equal status in income and education.

Finally, Julius proposed to her. Traditionally, the Ghanaian way was to ask the girl's father for her hand in marriage, but justice told him that it was up to her to say yes or no, that her father was thousands of miles away and, quite frankly, would not oppose his thirty-something daughter getting married. To Julius, this was sacrilegious; to marry a girl without her father's blessing was tantamount to stealing her, but knowing Justice's take on matters of feminism, he dared not put it that way lest she go ballistic, thinking that he was treating her like property. He gently told her that it was all up to her but it was an African tradition to have the blessing of the parents so that the marriage would be successful. Julius was known for applying such diplomacy in these types of cases, whether to close a large banking deal or convince a reluctant prospective lifelong partner, and it did work for Justice, who, after all, wanted to marry him and also have a long-lasting successful marriage.

Justice told him that he could call her dad if he felt it was necessary. Julius told Justice that this was not a matter to bring up in a phone call across the Atlantic and the proper way to handle things was to meet her father face to face. Justice was shocked. The question was turning out to be a very expensive one. But she wanted to respect Julius's wishes, and after all, she was due to visit home and see her parents anyway.

They flew to North Carolina by way of Washington and rented a car to drive to Greensboro. Justice remarked that although they could have flown there faster, she wanted to show Julius the country of the East Coast of the United States, so they made the almost six-hour drive after one night of rest in Northern Virginia. Justice's parents lived in the suburbs of Greensboro. Her mother was a retired librarian who, at an early age, had instilled in her children the importance of books and how fundamental reading was in education and success in life as a whole. Her father was a truck driver who was on the road a lot to support the family, but when he was home, he was very involved in his children's lives.

Justice had already told her parents that she'd met a potential husband in Ghana and how insistent he was about meeting them formally, and her mother had arranged a dinner for the couple on a Friday evening. They exchanged cordial niceties, and by the end of the evening, both parents were very impressed with Julius. They especially appreciated how deferential he was to them in asking for their daughter's hand in marriage. The couple did not know that there were still men who gave that much thought about what the girl's parents thought about such a decision, which was all up to the prospective couple, but they thanked Julius nonetheless. Julius, in response, was elated that he was now a legitimate future son-in-law. After spending a few more days in North Carolina, the pair continued on their mini-vacation/engagement party to the West Coast and flew to Northern California's Napa Valley and wine country. Justice was a huge wine aficionado, and she wanted Julius to formally propose there.

They built a lovely life together in Ghana and continued on to much more success in their professional lives as well. So, Justice took many other roles in marketing Ghana and West Africa in general for those young, professional African American females who were disenchanted with romance-less and stressful lives in America. She told Nikki that in addition to her nine-to-five job at the financial district of Accra, she'd also started an online dating website exclusively intended for African Americans looking for African husbands or wives. She suggested to Nikki that any young African American college graduate who had not yet gotten married should check out her site. Justice told Nikki that she and her husband had been happily married for seven years and now had three boys. She said that she never had an ounce of worries that her sons were going to be hurt by the police in Ghana, but she would be hysterical if she had to raise her boys in America. Justice mentioned how the movie *Queen & Slim*, in which a successful lawyer and her date are forever destroyed because of the abuse of one police officer who feels that unlawfully beating on a young black man is going to make him a bigger man;. had forever changed her view about the police.

Nikki explained that those African Americans who started their new lives in Africa were not only those in their productive stages of life, but retirees as well. Nikki contacted many of them, wanting to know everything: the good, the bad, and the ugly of living in Africa and leaving the country in which they were born and raised. She had so many personal questions that she wanted unearthed before making a final decision, including why they had left the US, what obstacles they faced in their new adopted country, and how the cultural differences and new way of life affected them. She interviewed those with kids as well as those without, the married couples and singles. She wanted to make sure she had a complete understanding of what living in Africa was like.

After meeting and interviewing many successful Americans who had migrated to Africa, Nikki found out that one of the major reasons why the overwhelming numbers of those who had moved to Africa to live had decided to leave America was due to mistreatment and racism they had faced. Many had left because they felt America had gotten much worse with the election of Donald J. Trump, that the racism and unfairness that had always been in America was given more legitimacy with his coming to the White House and Trump was only fanning a flame that had already been under the surface.

Others indicated that the violence against blacks in America was just too much for them to handle, and they wanted to be where they felt safe and secure. Others saw opportunity in Africa, and they wanted to be the first to be there. They saw Africa as the next frontier. Some also saw Africa as the next oil-rich Middle East; the only difference was that Africa had more gold, silver, and other minerals than the Middle East countries ever had.

# 6

# EXPERIENCE AFRICA

*"An Artist must be free to choose what he does, certainly, but he must also never be afraid to do what he might choose."* **Langston Hughes**

Once Nikki had gotten all the answers she wanted to hear, the next step in her project was how to share this information with her like-minded professional group of intellectual friends. Her idea was to create a support group that discussed the idea of professional African Americans who could come up with a plan where, if it became necessary for the African Americans to consider leaving America for the motherland, there was a strategy. She knew her close friends Dr. Khalid, who was born in Africa, Elmer, and Richard had had their own experiences with being black professionals in America, that they all had described the racial trauma they'd experienced directly or indirectly.

She knew that the four of them could, through their individual and collective knowledge, be a helpful support system for those considering the idea of relocating.

Nikki arranged a group discussion and had everyone describe their take on the issue. Dr. Khalid had already invited Albert and his family, who were eager to hear out the discussion. The family had already heard about the group and wanted to contribute their ideas. Albert suggested that to get visibility for the group and their ideas, they include Chad in the discussion. With his access to journalists, he could get the word out about the group's plans. Nikki was initially reluctant, but she was convinced by Dr. Khalid and others that having different points of view would help garner wide-ranging support for the group. Having Albert and Hilda in the discussion would broaden its scope. Because the black experience in America has no borders when it comes to class—a black doctor, businessman, or politician is treated the same as an unemployed black man—the need to be as inclusive as possible was of prime importance.

It was obvious to all that due to continued killings of blacks at the hands of the police, the problem of murdering innocent, unarmed citizens was no longer tolerable. For those who were fortunate enough not to die in a police shooting, the trauma of abuse and the mishandled justice system was worse than death itself. They agreed that being in America as a black person put a target on one's back. Earning a lot of money, getting a degree, or establishing a professional career did not make you immune. Being a veteran was not going to shield you. Being rich and famous was not going to prevent an uneducated policeman from disrespecting you. Even United States congressmen and women complained about being unfairly pulled over by the police while they drove. Those who could afford nice cars were asked if they had stolen those vehicles, and the unwarranted searches performed with "stop and frisk" in one of the most famous cities in the world, New York City, under Mayor Michael Bloomberg caused a trauma of their own.

After several people among the original members of the group had expressed their views on African American migration back to the homeland, the new members, including Mr. Albert's family and Chad, the journalist, were introduced to the forum.

Albert explained to the group that even though he did not have the education and expertise, he'd had his share of experiences living in America and its heartless treatment of the black people. He said that he had been working for the local hospital for over twenty-five years, and every time he had been promised a supervisory promotion, it had been given to a much less experienced and always white younger individual. He said it never failed to amaze him how that same individual was then trained by him to perform their duties. He finally gave up and just started counting the days before retirement. He held on so that his girls could finish their education.

His wife, Hilda, expressed the same frustration. She reported that it had taken her close to two decades to reach the supervisory position at her workplace because, like Albert, whenever she was up for a promotion, they gave it to a white employee, one with less experience and the same level of education, if not less. She said she could not accept this maltreatment anymore and complained to the human resources department, at which point the company finally gave up, as they were worried that she would take legal action.

Lisa, who was in her last year of law school, then took the floor. She described how rampant discrimination was in her first two years of law school. She shared with the group how even the academic advisors treated black students differently; in a way, they were trying to break African American students to the point that they quit law school entirely. She suggested to the doctors in the meeting that the medical profession should come up with a new condition or ailment, either physical or mental, that diagnosed the health risks associated with institutional racism and discrimination. She said she had seen people suffering from unfair treatment in the workplace because of the color of their skin.

She had also seen some of her medical-student friends of color being mistreated by their professors and classmates. Many of those future black doctors had been told directly or indirectly, both by their peers as well as their professors, how they had been admitted to medical school because of affirmative action and how their intellects or abilities were not the basis of their selection, but quotas. Never mind that those black students had to take the same medical school entrance exams, that they had to study long hours, just like their white counterparts. Never mind how most of those minority students did not have the wealthy parents that their white schoolmates did or the legacy admissions that favored the white privileged doctors' kids so they were given a free pass for admission.

Those young minds were forever impacted by such horrible treatment. Some of them had been the first in their families to even go to college. Their parents had to work multiple jobs to be able to help their kids finish school. Lisa reported how she had suffered the bullying and abuse of white privileged law school mates, who had sarcastically asked her if she was going to work for the NAACP (National Association for the Advancement of Colored People), the ACLU (American Civil Liberty Union), or some other organization that has to do with public legal aid. The insinuation was that a black lawyer was not going to be able to work at a well-known, high-paying New York or Washington, DC, law firm, that no matter the caliber of the law school they attended, they would only end up in a mediocre position.

In a way, the students underlined and magnified the racism that was apparent in the halls of higher education in America. They testified without knowing it that no matter how great a black lawyer was, they would never be given the equal opportunity they deserved in the land.

Lisa continued her explanation; "The only way those of us who received so much hate and merciless discrimination were able to continue was that we had the prize right in front of us. If we did not keep looking at the prize of graduating and doing so with distinction, then we would let them win. So, we had to bootstrap to overcome that type of hazing and abuse." Lisa attested to the fact that not everyone could withstand that type of bullying and only God knew how many black students at all levels of higher education and professional school had given up altogether due to such institutional racism.

After her passionate speech, she introduced her fiancé, Chad, to the group. She told the members that although Chad was white, and from a privileged family at that, she had known him for a long time before their relationship and he had always been someone who had shown great sympathy towards the minorities. She told them of the many protests for justice and equality he had participated in, that sometimes he knew more than her about what has been going on socially in all parts of the country. She explained how racism had exploded like a brushfire since the election of Donald Trump and how Chad had access to more information due to his connections as a journalist. She said that Chad would be a great asset to promote changes that the country needed since not everyone could emigrate from their homeland.

Lisa was a firm believer that America was for Americans, including blacks. She stressed her opinion that leaving America because of its mistreatment of African Americans was not the only solution, that blacks had built this country and invested in it physically, emotionally, and financially. Leaving or running away, as some might view it, would be silly in her opinion. She felt that the men and women who had died or been imprisoned for the equality and freedom of blacks in America would not appreciate it if their blood and treasures were wasted by giving up and running away to Africa rather than fighting on and continuing to struggle for their rightful piece of the American pie.

She argued for the idea of reparations, where every African American living in America who could trace their ancestors to slavery would be given an investment voucher to start a small business. This would be different from cash sent from the Treasury Department; it would be a business opportunity where the Small Business Administration would help people come up with a valid startup needed in their community. For instance, those black neighborhoods designated as food desert areas would have community-owned grocery stores. Such a community investment could be a win-win situation both for the business owners and the residents, who could get their needed groceries without going too far. That could also contribute to well-nourished kids in the neighborhood, leading to well-educated kids whose parents were not worried about food insecurity. That type of community investment, Lisa thought, was going to trickle down to other sectors, and those who were against the payment of reparations for crimes committed centuries ago could understand that community re-investment was going to benefit everyone.

After a long pause, Lisa apologized for taking so much time and handed the microphone to Chad.

Chad and Lydia, the wife of Dr. Michael and the mother of Jamal, were the only white people in the forum, but they had their own differences. Chad thanked everyone for allowing him to join the meeting. He underlined the fact that any forum was only as great as how well the members listened to each other's point of view. He told the group that even though members could have different ways of looking at issues facing the African American community, the ultimate goal was to find a long-lasting and positive solution to those social problems. He expressed his complete understanding that he was never going to fully put his feet in the shoes of his African American friends but that he had always been supportive of equal justice for all. He shared with the group the article he'd written about the leak of the administration's lack of care for minority groups negatively affected by COVID-19.

He understood that some members might view him as an outsider without a complete understanding of what black Americans felt, but he was willing to take a lot of heat from some strong-minded individuals who were of the opinion that the only way to eliminate the threat of abuse and discrimination was to leave this land for good, a land they had always belonged to. Chad did not want to attempt to sway anyone nor change any minds; he simply wanted to show that he could be a medium of communication for the group. He could use his ability to shed light on this new group so that they could at least become more visible on social media platforms as well as in the higher education arena, where new ideas are exchanged among the future decision-makers of tomorrow.

Those who were in the pro-migration group were aware of the importance of building allies among like-minded individuals so long as they were instrumental in sharing information and collaborating on shedding light on the issues faced by the blacks in America; in that regard, Chad was very willing to help.

Both Albert and Hilda were inclined to disagree with their daughter, Lisa, about staying put in America and not succumbing to defeat. However, they did not want to put their daughter on the spot.

Sabrina, the younger daughter of Albert and Hilda, was studying journalism, and she had a different and strong opinion. She was by far the most militant when it came to the option of migrating to Africa. She vehemently disagreed with her lawyer sister that black America should just sit and wait for things to change. Sabrina pointed out that contrary to what many had hoped, after the election of Barak Obama, things had only gotten much worse for black folks. Sabrina was of the opinion that Obama's two terms had created more hate and racism against blacks. Of course, this did not happen in a vacuum; the fire of racism against Obama was fanned by the birther conspiracy that was started by Donald Trump. However, Sabrina underlined the fact that although the recently enacted laws requiring the police to wear cameras had uncovered some crimes by them against black citizens, no one really knew how many police shootings and brutalities went unreported. Sabrina agreed with those who wanted to consider moving back to Africa to at least check it out. She pointed out that if things could get better for those who decided to move, as was described by the overwhelming majority of those who had already settled there, then doing the same would be worthy of consideration.

Sabrina had another reason to argue for the idea of migrating to Africa. Unbeknownst to the rest of the group, she wanted to travel there to find a future husband. She did not beat around the bush about it at all. She pointed out that there weren't many brothers in America to choose from. She said they were either in jail, unemployed, or unable to handle a successful, educated, and opinionated black sister. She shared with the group how many of her girlfriends had traveled there and met nice African men who adored them and treated them like queens.

Nikki sat there, laughing her brains out, knowing that that dating website created by Justice really was reaching out across the Atlantic faster than the speed of light. It appeared that Nikki's argument was being easily made by Sabrina. Throughout human history, people had moved from one place to another for a variety of reasons. For some, it was to find freedom of religion, like the Puritans of Massachusetts. For others, it was economic freedom, like those who migrated to America in the middle of the 1800s due to the Irish Potato Famine. Sabrina's point was a valid one indeed: one should always be free to pursue a life full of romance, lifelong companionship, and happiness.

Lydia, who had come along with her husband, Dr. Michael, was completely against the idea; she and Nikki had always been at odds ever since Lydia had married Michael, who had become very aloof and distant from the entire family. Nikki knew her brother was always loving, but she blamed Lydia for destroying the close-knit family. Somehow the two women had come to view each other as archenemies. Lydia had come to torpedo Nikki's whole idea. She viewed Africa as a backward country, not realizing that there were over fifty countries on the African continent.

Lydia was a very feisty and unapologetic person. When it came to reparations, she pointed out that slavery did not start with Africa but had been around since the dawn of history, and today's white people should not be punished for what had been done hundreds of years ago. As a white woman with black children, Lydia was very adamantly against her race paying for the damages of her forefathers to her own children. This was the mother of all moral crises.

Nikki sat in a corner, trying hard to contain herself, while Lydia, who didn't care that her husband and son were in the audience, continued her sermon, asking when this country would come to the realization that people should not always go back to what happened centuries ago. She had forgotten that her own son had almost been killed because of the color of his skin.

Lydia was not only against the idea of reparations; she actually did not realize the economic disparity that existed in America. Perhaps marrying a black cardiologist had led her to believe that every American family was as well off as she was. Even Chad, who came from a wealthy white family, was shocked to hear what Lydia was saying. Her reason for opposing the idea of relocating to Africa was that all African countries were undeveloped and backward. She could not fathom the idea of leaving this perfect country to live where there was no running water or electricity. Dr. Michael did not utter a word, but his face said it all. He was extremely uncomfortable about what his wife was saying and how she was belittling the whole group with such distasteful remarks. Nikki felt for her big brother and, with her facial expressions, let him know that all was well.

In addition to Lisa, Chad, and Lydia, Richard was also adamantly against the idea of African American migration. He agreed with Lisa that this land was their land, that it was the hard work of their forefathers who had built the plantations, the highway system, the railroads, and everything else. He believed that by leaving their homeland, America, they would be handing over their dignity. This country was as much theirs as those who claimed to be the majority, those who kept saying, "Make America great again," and there was no way in hell he was going to allow that to happen. Richard even suggested that every black man and woman of legal age buy guns to defend themselves, especially now that America had become more armed than ever before.

Richard's take on the matter of reparations was much different than Lisa's. His was to demand full cash from the United States Treasury; in his mind, this was the least that the US government could do to undo the wrongs of slavery and the centuries of abuse and inequalities. He stressed that no amount of cash was going to do any justice for the abuse, murder, rape, and destruction of generations, but at least those who were still living could make a life for themselves and catch the progress and dream they had been denied for generations.

Apart from Lisa, Chad, and Richard, the rest of the group was unanimous in their agreement that, for those professionals who could afford to uproot their families to Africa, it was not only worth considering, but was a must. Lydia was in a league of her own.

The reason the majority of the group was in agreement was that they realized that Trump winning the election again was irrelevant. The damage was already done. Black voters were harassed to prevent them from casting their votes, and the next thing would be the reinstatement of Jim Crow laws. In their own ways, each member of the group had experienced the bad taste of racism in America, and the thought of putting their kids through the danger of police abuse was even more difficult than their own experiences.

With all that considered, however, Dr. Khalid, who, as mentioned before, was the only one born in Africa, wanted to present a cautious tone to the group. He wanted everyone to be aware that Africa had its own problems and that, both mentally and emotionally, one must be ready for some disappointments. He said that there was still rampant corruption in Africa and those who expected a smooth transition might be unpleasantly disappointed. He also pointed out that Africa is very undeveloped and those who were used to nicely kept highways and dependable municipal services would find the rudimentary systems there mediocre at best.

The flip side of those inconveniences was that there were business and developmental opportunities to create functional systems that would benefit all. The new talent from America and Europe could harness those opportunities, while the locals could benefit from the jobs and businesses created in the process. There was the chance to build interstate highway systems just like those in America, as well as railroads from Cairo to Cape Town that could run across Africa from north to south.

The key recommendation that Dr. Khalid pointed out was that anyone who decided to move there must have a business plan and clear strategy to implement it. As someone who regularly traveled to the continent, he'd found that there were many untapped diamond-in-the-rough opportunities, especially for the younger generations, so introducing African American college students to those prospects would be a great idea. He pointed out that if the Chinese and Indians were coming to Africa in record numbers, what was stopping African

Americans from doing so?

The floor was given to Nikki to share her experiences, as she had the most insight into the lives of those who had already resettled in West Africa. Nikki presented her heartfelt take on the idea of moving to Africa. She described her experience in Africa as stress-free and relaxed. This was also evident in those who had moved there from the States and how simpler their lives had become.

To eliminate any bias, Nikki only mentioned the African Americans who had actually moved to Africa. She did not want to present the feelings of African natives because that would create an impartial evaluation of the conditions on the ground. The most important advantage expressed by those who had moved to Africa was the sense of security and the feeling of being among family. Because everyone looked like them, even if they did not speak the same language, it gave them a self-assurance that they lacked in America. They did not feel followed by the police; the police provided an extra level of confidence and security rather than threaten their civil liberties. When they shopped in malls and expensive stores, they did not feel foreign; no salesclerk followed them around the store. They were addressed as "sir" and "madam." Business owners appreciated their business and did not fear them. Their neighbors looked out for them and greeted them with genuine feelings of love and coexistence, not a fake "hi" and "bye," like in America, where people have no time for each other.

Those who worked full time and those who had retired had the same level of contentment with their lives. There was no mortgage to worry about, as most people paid off their homes. There was no car payment, as the continent was cash for service. The system created was that you spent what you could afford; there was no systemic pressure to spend, which led to a stress-free community. She pointed out the success stories of Dr. Nightingale, the dentist, and Justice, to name a few. She told Sabrina that she had nothing to worry about, that her romance expedition would indeed be fulfilled; she just had to take the first step of checking out Africa.

Those with special skills could create businesses that were in demand. Doctors could create clinics and hospitals. Educators could set up schools and educational institutions. Lawyers could create law firms and consulting companies. By far, engineers and architects were in the greatest demand. Africa would need massive infrastructure improvements: roads, bridges, rail stations, hospitals, and schools. She reiterated how the entire continent would need a full-blown construction plan. The European colonizers had not added anything to the development of Africa. They had only stolen natural and human resources from the continent.

Nikki told her friends about the safety and security that moving to Africa provided to those African Americans who immigrated there, and she unveiled for them the proud history of the continent and the cultures within it, which African Americans were never taught about at schools. The fact that, before the so-called Western civilization that filled the American educational system's textbooks, the real civilizations started in Africa. Contrary to Donald Trump's name-calling, Africa was the home of the pharaohs of Egypt, the kingdom of Aksum in Ethiopia's Tigray region, the greatest civilization of the ancient world once between the Persian and Roman empires. She mentioned the history of the kingdom of Kush in what is now Sudan and which stood as a regional power on the banks of the River Nile for over a thousand years. The Mali Empire was another historic civilization in the western part of Africa that was remarkable in its education and record keeping. This cultural discovery, intentionally hidden from African Americans, reignited returnees' identity.

In terms of future advancement, Nikki pointed out to her audiences that the African American returnees saw a virgin landscape for investments. They also saw a population explosion that was going to need goods and services. Nikki mentioned that according to the United Nations, Africa has the highest rate of population growth, and sub-Saharan Africa is projected to double by the year 2050. Africa has sixty percent of the world's arable land. With food resources forecasted to become in short supply as world populations grow exponentially, Africa will be the basket of the world, as most of its agricultural land has not been farmed yet.

Those African Americans in the motherland saw a business opportunity that they had never envisioned. They had always been consumers of the Western propaganda that Africa was the continent of hunger and civil wars, coups and counter-coups, that there was nothing good about sub-Saharan Africa. But they realized the continent's immense developmental need.

Nikki gave a great example of how citizens of other countries were pouring into Africa. The Chinese, who invested in Africa's developmental projects, saw the gold mine and had beaten Americans and Europeans in cultivating relationships with African countries. The Turks have done the same recently. Indians had started to venture into the area as well. She presented the advantages that African Americans had over those other groups when it came to investing in Africa. The culture and homogeneity of African Americans was a huge asset. The locals would treat an African American as one of them. The color of their skin, which had been a liability in America, had, ironically, become a huge asset in the motherland. They had flipped that Trump mantra of making America great again to making Africa great again by moving there and making great lives for themselves and the natives.

Elmer asked about the disadvantages of moving to a new culture and how difficult it was for those who did to fit in. Sort of poking at Nikki, he told her that she was only showing everyone a rosy picture of the African continent, but he wanted to know everything. He pointed out that he had been there as a visitor a long time ago, during his college years. Back then, he would never have considered moving there, but with how bad America had gotten since the election of Donald Trump and the dangerous encounter his son had had with the police, he and his wife had started talking about the prospect of moving to Africa.

To answer those inquiries, Nikki was very frank. Based on what those who had settled in Africa had reported to her, it was not all hunky-dory all the time, especially during the initial transition. One of the initial shocks was the poor infrastructure, such as bad roads and bridges and unreliable electricity. Another problem was the lack of reliable public services, such as ambulance systems and vehicle emergency services.

However, the flipside of this was that there was an opportunity to develop a business solution. For those who were willing to take a chance on the continent, there was a wide array of untapped niches. Every one of those professional African Americans who had started the debate had a chance to make it big if they considered moving there. Nikki pointed out that, in fact, those who had incorporated business in Africa had done so much better than they would have in the States. Access to capital from local banks, which trusted the ingenuity and knowledge of black Americans, was much greater than in America.

Furthermore, the skills they had were in high demand. At the front of the line for those in demand were engineers and health care workers. The two most instrumental factors that attracted business-minded individuals were the affordable labor force and minimal taxation. Both of these usually contributed to the success of any type of investment, as they minimized the cost of doing business. What this led to was the growth and expansion of startups, not only in the capital cities, where so many were employed, but also in regional cities.

The feeling of those successful business owners was that they had not only succeeded in Africa, but they had also made its younger generations successful. It was a win-win situation.

As Nikki concluded her long but convincing presentation, she realized that it was time to implement the plan she had been making for so long. Right on the spot, she declared that she was now ready to share her final decision of packing and moving to Ghana, her ancestors' land, to make a life and career there. With palpable emotion, she pointed out that she was not going to raise a family in this country, where, after four hundred years, she was still unsure if she was welcome, where her stepbrother was brutally executed by the police and they still got away with it, where her nephew was almost killed because an officer thought a black teenager driving his father's expensive car must have stolen it, perhaps from a white owner, because a black person in the twenty-first century could not own such a luxurious vehicle.

While her nephew had not been killed, it had been a close call, and the young man had been killed emotionally. His whole outlook on life in America had been shattered because of the abuse and dehumanization of the encounter and how the police had gotten away with it all. It had created an indelible mark on such a young and impressionable mind forever. She imagined that if an upper-class physician's child could be treated that way, how would young inner-city black men without access to expensive attorneys fare in such an unjust world?

Nikki told everyone in the group and those who were following her online that she was going to stay in touch with them and be their ambassador in Africa. She went ahead with the plan and informed her family that she was moving to Accra, Ghana, and had already accepted a position at one of the major hospitals in the city. Her physician brother was initially concerned, but knowing his sister, he realized that trying to dissuade her from moving there was going to be an exercise in futility.

So, everyone gave her their blessings. Her nephew Jamal asked his father if he could go with his aunt and check out how things were in Africa. To sell the idea like a hotcake, he suggested that he could help her with the housework, gardening, and keeping an eye on African men who might find her beautiful and lonely. His aunt thought the idea was fabulous. His mother, of course, was scared about him going all the way to Africa, and granted, a mother will always look out for the best interests of her child. At the same time, most of the concern had to do with the stereotypical idea Americans had about Africa. She thought that he would be living in a hut and that conditions there would be terrible. She mentioned how some people who moved there from the developed world were infected with malaria and other tropical diseases, and she was concerned about Jamal getting sick.

Jamal's father, who hadn't been too keen initially about the idea of sending his son to Africa, went completely the other way. Lydia's disparaging attitude towards Africa had struck a nerve with him. He remembered how her disrespectful remarks had made other people feel at the meeting. He told his wife that her son had almost been killed by the county police who were hired to protect him, that he would rather have his son live in a hut in Africa than get killed or emotionally abused by the police in America. As for the diseases that the mother was worried about, he said that Jamal could actually pump up his immunity by traveling and getting a little bit of diarrhea and dysentery here and there. It was only going to toughen him up a little. He kind of applied the Somali proverb that said, "Ragga Socodku Waw door, Haduu mawdku daayee," "For young men, traveling is beneficial so long as death is delayed in the process."

He told Nikki to take her nephew with her so he could decide for himself. Besides, Jamal was not going to college that year, anyway. As a result of the extreme depression that was brought on by the traumatic experience with the police, he could not even leave the house nor drive. He was paranoid that he was going to run into another abusive police officer. Instead, Jamal had decided to take a gap year to explore other options. The opportunity to travel and see different places and meet different people was very appealing to him.

This was a huge plus for Nikki—not that she needed the company of a man to make the transition to Africa, as she had traveled there and made friends with the natives, but she was going to introduce a young generation of Americans to test-drive the idea of relocating to the motherland. She was like a religious figure with a group of non-believers who were suddenly leaning towards believing. For Nikki, this was a huge success, and she knew that Jamal was the type of person who would get along well there. He had a personality like hers, the kind of rebellious attitude that forced some kids to do what their parents disapproved of.

So, Jamal became Nikki's companion; he told his aunt that his mother would paint them all white if she could and that he wanted to go where he would be treated based on his true identity. The family agreed and gave Nikki and Jamal their blessing.

Before Nikki left for Africa, she created an international non-profit organization with her nephew: Experience Africa. This organization was tailored for young people of African descent who were interested in learning about Africa and the history of Pan-Africanism. She wanted to plant the seeds for the future generation, to teach Afro-Americans, Afro-Caribbeans, and others interested in Africa that there were opportunities in sub-Saharan Africa, that if they wanted economic and investment opportunities or freedom from police brutality, they had a home in Africa.

The interest for this organization was huge, and membership skyrocketed. Jamal became the point of contact for African American youths and was able to network with tens of thousands of high school and college Americans and Canadians who thought the idea was just fabulous. The age of Facebook, Instagram, Twitter and Snapchat made it easy to market and increase group membership; up-to-the-minute discussion groups were always on the cusp of any new developments.

As soon as Nikki and Jamal settled in Accra, they hit the ground running. Nikki had already secured a position at the University Teaching Hospital as an associate professor by day, and she'd also opened a part-time private clinic with a group practice. She brought to Africa the concept of nurse practitioner, and she also started teaching as an adjunct professor at the School of Social Work, where she introduced the concept of patient advocate. in America, she had identified patient care disparities among white privileged and minority patients. She knew that while, in America, the disparities might have been based on color, humans are the same in many aspects and, in Africa, the quality of patient care could be based on income and status. She wanted to teach new African doctors that care for patients should be boundless irrespective of the patient's social standing.

She introduced to the University Hospital a new position that was not in existence before, patient advocate, so the patient's bill of rights would be protected. The patients would be represented by their advocate, who would provide communication between them and the caregiver. In the event of patient incapacitation, that same advocate would act as the bridge between loved ones and caregivers so the patient's best interest was always at heart. The patient advocate was to be independent of the hospital so their job was secure and their salary was not controlled by doctors. This elimination of conflict of interest allowed every patient to receive the best possible care without any consideration of color, creed, faith, or income. The new concept also allowed doctors to be doctors without unnecessarily being bogged down by other social issues. It assured that there would be a standard of care and every provider was giving the best possible care to all patients.

Jamal started attending college in Ghana, and he gradually came back to his former self as he substantially recovered from the depression he had been suffering from while in the States. The sunny weather and living right next to the beach had a lot to do with it, too, but he also found a sense of belonging in Africa. He was no longer afraid of getting in trouble with the police. Ironically, the only police he ran into in Ghana were nice and, if anything, as curious about this young American as he was about them, and they welcomed him to the Gold Coast.

Jamal made friends both with locals as well as the Americans who had moved to Africa and those who had parents working for the foreign offices and other international organizations. The Experience Africa Organization, which he and his aunt spearheaded, had spread all over the world. It had even attracted Africans who lived in the Arabian countries who found the idea of African repatriation very appealing.

Back in America, Elmer and Dr. Khalid kept in contact with Nikki; the more they heard from her, the more they felt they needed to pack and move to Africa, too, as the conditions in the US were not getting any better for young blacks. As they both were raising teenagers, it was becoming more and more worrisome to live in the America of Donald Trump and his Senate cronies. Although many members of the forum were of the opinion that after Trump was voted out, America would be better, what they did not understand was that Trump had only exacerbated the race issue that had already been present in America. He had only unveiled the festering social problems that others had been hiding and lying about, not to mention that almost half of America had voted for him regardless of all his negativity.

The Experience Africa organization was really the last straw for both Elmer and Dr. Khalid, as their children had become members of the organization. One of the obstacles for those professionals who had thought of moving to Africa because of the living conditions they found themselves in had always been the worries of what their children, who had been born in America, would say about such a drastic move. However, the Experience Africa organization had made it so appealing to young people that moving to Africa was a fashionable thing. Tracing back their roots was not backward thinking after all, and sharing identity was as important as existing at times.

For the grownups, especially those who were not born in America, like Dr. Khalid, the issue of race and implied racism was not clear. Their loyalty to the idea of success in the New World outweighed their worry about the conditions on the ground. They were busy trying to make it in their quest to achieve the American dream, while their kids, who were born into this American debacle of indirect discrimination, unveiled by the four years of the Donald Trump presidency, understood how they were mistreated by the system irrespective of their parents' success. Those black children of immigrants identified more with their African American cohorts than their parents did as naturalized Americans.

While it is worth pointing out that immigrant parents were not blind to the experience of discrimination themselves, their primary mission was to make it in America, to provide better opportunities for their American-born children, and they had. They never imagined, however, that their kids would be more Afrocentric than themselves, that the American-born children of African immigrants would want to consider moving back to where their parents had come from. So, when their kids approached them about the idea of relocating to Africa, even on a temporary basis, the parents were ecstatic. It seemed as though the unveiled, normalized racism and overt discrimination of the Trump presidency had emboldened white supremacists, who heaved their flags and swastikas, and this was the catalyst that precipitated the idea of leaving America for the motherland.

Both Dr. Khalid and Elmer continued to research how to make the move to Africa. They were already sold on the idea, but they wanted to take their kids on the tour and let them see for themselves before the decision was finalized. Richard, who was managing a real estate firm and was also interested in the idea, could not come along, but he was kept in the loop.

Sabrina, who had graduated from journalism school, had contacted Nikki and Justice and planned to be part of the trip, too. She wanted to explore the idea of networking with some international media companies there for employment. So, the tour group was very diverse. Nikki arranged an elaborate tour for the families as well as the single members; she introduced them to Ghana's immigrant communities from the US, UK, and other European countries. She wanted to show the group how moving to Africa had benefitted those immigrants and contributed to the development of the continent. Nikki was able to network with multiple successful companies, startups initiated by immigrants. Among those that had really taken off were medical labs, hospitals, daycare centers, educational institutions from pre-K to college, hospitality companies and media/television businesses. She showcased construction companies and architectural firms that had blended with local companies to collaborate on infrastructure developments in Western and Central African countries.

The youths had their own tour, which coincided with a world conference of the Experience Africa organization. Young people from high school seniors to college graduates attended the conference, coming all the way from Australia, Canada, the United States, and the United Kingdom. The major factor that brought all those young people was not the desire to travel and explore the world, but to redefine their identity. Most had grown up in communities that did not value them, and while their parents had done well to give them great education and comfortable lives, they could not provide the sense of belonging the youths yearned for in the Americas and other Western countries. What they felt in Africa with people who looked like them and thought like them was magic. They felt like they had come HOME. They realized that the idea that Africa is a shithole, as described by Donald Trump, is far from the truth. Accra had everything that young and trendy kids in the West could ever want: malls, restaurants, movie theaters, and gyms. In some aspects, they realized that Africa was more advanced than the West in terms of mobile money transfer and easy banking options. They were also not worried about not going to a certain neighborhood or being fearful of the police.

Sabrina reconnected with Nikki and Justice, with whom she had been communicating for some time before coming for the tour. Justice told Sabrina that she had connections for potential employment for her with the West Africa branch of the BBC in Accra and that if Sabrina was fine with making the move, she could arrange a meeting with the group. Sabrina was beyond shocked—but extremely excited. She told Justice and Nikki that she would love to consider the move if she was offered the job. Justice told Sabrina that she would ask her husband to make the arrangement with one of his best friends, who was a senior Africa correspondent with the BBC. Sabrina was so happy that she was even being considered by such a well-known media conglomerate as the BBC. Nikki told her to calm down a bit, as the deal wasn't done yet.

The tour for the parents included meetings with members of the business community and the chamber of commerce to introduce investment collaborations that could be made with prospective immigrants from the developed world. Nikki introduced Dr. Khalid to the state-of-the-art clinics in Accra, but more importantly, she showed him how much demand there was for specialists and American-trained physicians. With the growth in oil and gas production in West Africa, the upward mobility of the masses had been accelerating, and people had started to care more about preventive health, so well-equipped clinics with highly skilled providers were sought after. Dr. Khalid's eyes were opened to the potential that existed in Ghana for health care delivery as well as insurance for the middle class.

In terms of finance and business, Julius, the vice president of one of Ghana's largest banks, told them of the loan services offered by local banks and how willing and ready those banks were to attract international investments. Elmer, with his background in accounting and finance, was the one who was gathering the most pertinent information for the rest of the visitors from America, and he was extremely impressed at the generosity of some of the concessions those banks were offering for doing business in Ghana.

On the other side, the city of Accra showcased large companies in its convention center to facilitate network interactions between the local businesses and those interested in moving to and doing business in the city. Those local business owners knew that they needed the knowledge and expertise that many of those immigrants would bring with them.

The visitors, including the families of Dr. Khalid and Elmer, left Ghana with a very positive impression: that Africa was going to be the place to be for the twenty-first century and beyond. It was a continent with a vibrant future, explosive population growth, and untapped natural resources. They realized that the new gold rush was going to be in Africa, and no other group was better equipped than those who started the process of moving there first. Not only was the idea sold to the parents, but the youths were more enthusiastic about relocation, as, naturally, they were more risk-takers.

What had become apparent to the younger generation, the leaders of the not-too-distant tomorrow, was that black people had always been disadvantaged all over the world. The youngsters, through reading history and literature, watching movies, and living in the West, where they had been raised, realized that blacks had always held the short end of the stick. No matter if they were in the minority, as in North America and Australia, or the majority, as in South Africa, the black race always suffered the most. The Experience Africa organization allowed those smart youngsters to convince their reluctant parents to realize the overwhelming potential for everlasting fairness and equity for blacks in their homeland: Africa.

Furthermore, the college graduates among the members of the organization, like Sabrina and her friends, firmly believed that they were going to be the developers of Africa. They resisted the idea that after the Western colonizers had already usurped the human as well as other natural resources of Africa in the past centuries, the Chinese and Indians would be the next in line to do the same. They wanted to take the lead in investing in Africa themselves before any outsiders came and raped the continent all over again. They believed, as Albert Einstein put it, that "doing the same thing over and over again and expecting different results is the definition of insanity." So, just as the leaders of Africa's sixties liberation movement had been energetic in removing the weight of colonialism, the young Africans planned to put their energy toward making Africa the next big success through investment projects and development.

Four days before the end of the tour, Sabrina received the invitation she was eagerly awaiting: the interview with the BBC. Justice made it happen. She planned a goodbye party for some of the tour group at her estate and included a side meeting for Sabrina to mingle with journalists from the BBC's Africa section. Sabrina was not prepared for interviews and had come to Africa for a preliminary tour, but she was serious about the prospect of moving there if the conditions were right and the opportunity presented itself. In Sabrina's mind, those conditions included a well-paying job, a great-looking Mr. Right, and a safe neighborhood.

As far as her sister, Lisa, was concerned, though, Africa was too oversold and, in a nutshell, all hat and no cattle. She told Sabrina over the phone that she could easily get a great referral from Chad, Lisa's fiancé, who, in his role as Washington correspondent, had a lot of connections in the media arena. However, Sabrina did not want them to think that she needed their help; she wanted to stand on her own, to find her own connections and network, so she told her older sister that, with all due respect, she was fine fending for herself.

When Sabrina received the interview notification, she never thought things were going to be lined up so smoothly. The BBC correspondent was a gentleman from Tunisia who spoke French, English, and Arabic, and he had traveled throughout the Middle East, Europe, and Africa for his job as an international reporter. His name was Jibril. He was looking for someone who was also eager for a new life and was interested in traveling. He asked Sabrina if she was okay with moving to Ghana to be a member of his team. She told him that traveling was one of her hobbies and doing it internationally was going to add more to her love for journalism. Jibril was not expecting an American girl who had never left her home country to be eager to travel.

After the formalities of the interview were done, Jibril wanted to test the international knowledge of this promising young journalist. This was not a unique line of questioning for Sabrina. To gauge the level of awareness of future media professionals, he always tested them quite rigorously. Jibril asked Sabrina if she could name a few notable female journalists, either locally or internationally.

She told him she was a huge fan of one of the most well-known and internationally respected journalists, who was once stationed in Accra for the American National Public Radio's Africa desk: Ofeibea

Quist-Arcton. She said she found Ofeibea to be the epitome of a professional journalist. She mentioned how she used to listen to NPR on her long ride to morning classes and how, whenever there was a story from Africa, the radio anchor would reach out to Ofeibia. After the news, the anchor would say, "Thank you, Ofeibia," to which Ofeibia always replied, "Always a pleasure." A second international correspondent that Sabrina shared with Jibril was Christiane Amanpour at the CNN headquarters in London. Sabrina said that both these heavyweight champions of the media were her heroes.

That sealed the deal, and Sabrina got the job. The package included a very generous salary, a brand-new bungalow in one of the most desirable areas of Accra, a car with or without chauffeur, based on her choice, thirty days of paid vacation, with two tickets to America each year, and many other benefits. Sabrina was blown away by the offer and accepted immediately.

As she was telling the deal to Lisa, the soon-to-be-lawyer told her younger sister that she had accepted the deal too soon, that she could have asked for more money or a sign-on bonus, but for Sabrina, that was too greedy, and she told her sister that she was happy with the decision she had made.

The next day, Jibril introduced Sabrina to the entire staff, and she was very well received. The plan was that she would go back to the States and start the process of moving to Accra. She was given three weeks to tie up any loose ends in America, plus two more weeks for getting acclimated to Ghana, i.e., getting proper documentation, driver's license, and other necessary paperwork to help her reside in Ghana.

The next step was for the parents to start the process of making the dream of relocating to Africa a reality. It was also the intention of the leadership of the Experience Africa organization to open branches in every historically black college and university to teach African American Students at a very young age the importance of reconnecting to Mother Africa.

Dr. Khalid and Elmer discussed what they had seen with those in the group who could not make the visit. As they were eagerly awaited by everyone, they presented an unfiltered report of what Africa had to offer. Nikki's brother, Michael, the cardiologist, wanted to know about the possibility of opening a cardiac specialty hospital there. Ever since his sister and son Jamal had left for Ghana, he had developed a keen interest in changing his venue. This idea was also influenced by the fact that his marriage to Lydia had fallen apart. Michael shared his situation with Dr. Khalid and Elmer, who had become his closest friends since the forum had been created.

He told them that he and Lydia had been facing very tough years due to multiple factors. He met Lydia while doing his residency. She came from a modest family in West Virginia. Being the first to leave home and go beyond high school, she went to a community college, where she was trained to be a respiratory therapist. In the community where she grew up, most kids did not complete high school; for her to have a job at a hospital after getting an associate's degree was a huge achievement. After meeting and falling in love with Dr. Michael, her life changed completely. Things got even better after he became a board-certified cardiologist, when nice homes and cars, vacations to places she'd only read about in magazines, and everything a rich doctor's wife wanted became available to her.

Dr. Michael told his friends that their marriage problems started with Lydia's uncontrollable spending. As a man who was raised to never spend beyond his means, Dr. Michael was not a materialistic man. He did provide for his family and sent his kids to great colleges, but he did not believe in wasting money. Lydia stopped working after the kids were born, and Dr. Michael wanted her to spend time raising the children, but after they were all grown up, he wanted her to go back to work and appreciate the value of work for a change. Lydia did not heed that advice; in her mind, there was a lot of money that her husband was bringing home, and there was no need for her to put in the extra nights and late hours required for a respiratory therapist to work at the hospital.

With no kids to raise and nothing to do all day long, Lydia had too much time on her hands. Even the housework was done by maids and housekeepers. With Dr. Michael gone all day between the hospital and his private clinic, Lydia joined a group of ladies in the same socioeconomic status who also had too much time in their hands. They started going on wine-tasting trips and shopping sprees. The entire week was sometimes spent on day trips to wineries and sightseeing. Dr. Michael would come home with nobody there and no dinner available. He would just eat whatever was available or order something. His sister, Nikki, told him multiple times that the least Lydia could do was have a healthy, warm dinner available for him after a long day of work since she had nothing to do all day, but Dr. Michael overlooked all that; he was not happy with it, but he did not want to fuss about it too much.

However, things got much worse with Lydia's spending and bad habits. Her wine-tasting club caused her to become dependent on alcohol. Drinking was no longer a habit of the high life; she became a full-blown alcoholic, to the point where the other members in her club started avoiding her. This rejection only created more dependency on wine. Dr. Michael advised her that she was going to need intervention or she would have very severe health consequences.

Lydia was a very stubborn person; she was always right, and everyone was wrong. The problem became apparent to the kids, although Dr. Michael tried to shield it from them. In hindsight, his mother's alcoholism, as well as the incident with the police, caused the depression that her son Jamal suffered from and his subsequent decision to leave home and go with his aunt Nikki to Africa.

Dr. Michael continued pouring his heart out to his sympathetic friends, Dr. Khalid and Elmer. He needed to get out of the mess. He told his friends that he had pleaded with Lydia to get help with her substance-abuse problem, but she was in severe denial. He said he even tried to get her family to get involved in an attempt to help her; unfortunately, most of them were also in the same predicament, if not worse. He said that after Jamal left, nothing else was keeping him at home, so before things could get any worse, he moved out of the house and filed for divorce.

Both Dr. Khalid and Elmer were heartbroken to hear Dr. Michael's situation, but he said he was happier now that he was moving on, and he really wanted to check out the possibilities of starting something in Ghana, where he could also join his sister and Jamal. Dr. Khalid shared with him that there was a huge market for high-end, American-style health care, and cardiology services were in demand. Dr. Khalid told Dr. Michael that due to the introduction of Western-style diets in Africa, heart disease and obesity had become more common, especially among affluent communities. Therefore, high-quality, specialized cardiac surgery and services had become hard to come by. Some European-trained cardiologists had set up clinics, but with such high demand, that was not sufficient. Those who could afford treatment elsewhere traveled to America and Europe, but if they could find well-trained specialists, they would prefer to seek care at home.

The question that Dr. Michael had was how to locate initial startup capital for a health care delivery system there. To that end, Elmer had done his share of exploring how to finance new businesses in West Africa. He shared with Dr. Michael how attractive some of the deals he had seen in Accra were. He told the doctor that he could basically build a whole new cardiac specialty hospital there and, with the type of upfront capital plus the business tax break and investment concessions that those banks were offering, it would be a no-brainer. From an accountant's perspective, the cost of doing businesses was next to nothing; with the tax advantage and almost zero interest rate, not to mention the proven success of health care businesses due to high level of demand, there were no cons to heading for Ghana to start a medical care business.

Elmer mentioned to both doctors that it would be even more sensible if the two could join forces and collaborate on a project. That would lessen the risk that the banks were going to assume, and perhaps the deal some of the banks were willing to offer would be more advantageous. Dr. Michael liked the idea of collaborating with Dr. Khalid, who would, as an internist, be the referral base for his future patients. Dr. Khalid also suggested that with Elmer's accounting background as well as finance and marketing experience under his belt, perhaps the three of them could create a health care company with multiple branches within the same umbrella. This would include an insurance services branch, a health care delivery system with clinics and outpatient surgery centers, preventive care clinic, and a hospital management system similar to those in America.

After a general agreement with the idea, they decided that they needed to write a business plan for the project. This business plan was going to be presented to three different banks in Ghana. After careful consideration, they would decide on the best offer. The three decided that the business would be shared amongst themselves with an equal amount of initial capital investment, and they decided to hire an independent attorney to draw out a corporate contractual agreement for three equal partners as soon as they got a preliminary offer from a bank.

Elmer took it upon himself to prepare the plan and communicate with the banks in Accra. After the business plan was approved by all parties, they made a conference call to each of the three banks they wanted to do business with. Dr. Michael requested that his intention to set up a business in Ghana be hidden from his sister and, by extension, his son. He wanted to surprise them by just showing up one day in Accra. Everyone agreed not to spill the beans.

After the conference call with the bank executives, they were told they would hear back in a week or so. Dr. Khalid, who was a bit skeptical about African promises, told the others that they should plan on a few weeks rather than a week. To their surprise, the first bank called three days after the meeting and made its offer. Obviously, this was the Commerce Bank, led by Julius, who was married to Justice, the New Yorker. Julius was well aware that the Americans were shopping for a good deal, and with cash just sitting in the savings, he wanted to offer a fat deal that they could not refuse. He also wanted to get into the American immigrant market before other banks in West Africa and get his bank's name out there.

Elmer and the doctors hired an international commerce attorney to look over the offer. Julius was basically giving away so much in this business offerings that the lawyer was blown away. He advised the three not to even think about this one and sign the deal. They did not want to appear too eager; besides, they still had to hear from the other two banks.

Two weeks passed, and they still hadn't heard back from the other banks. This was where Julius's understanding of the value Americans place on timeliness really paid off. As someone who had dealt with multiple American institutions over the years and was now married to an American wife who meticulously evaluated everything in the couple's life, Julius had a major advantage over his competition. He knew a prompt response would impress the newcomers.

After exactly two weeks, both banks responded with their offers. The Westbank Commercial Bank presented them with a deal like Julius's bank had offered; however, the rate was slightly higher. The Central Commercial Bank had the lowest rate, but terms of repayment were more stringent. Plus, it had not made the concessions that Julius was offering. After they considered everything, they decided on Julius's bank. This gave them more leeway, and as they had already developed a good relationship with Justice and Julius, they felt more comfortable doing business with them. The icing on the cake was the fact that Julius had agreed to give the prospective clients two months to consider the deal without increasing the rate or changing the terms of the contract. This was the time they needed to draw up the partnership contract. It also gave them enough time to mentally and emotionally get themselves and their families ready for this monumental task of moving and starting a new venture in Africa.

Perhaps going back to Ghana and spending some time evaluating the location of the company's headquarters and negotiating other required logistics was in order. They debated if asking for more time than the two months allotted was proper in light of all the concessions they had already been given. The doctors were more skeptical about pushing Julius any further and shied away from being too pushy. However, having an accountant and numbers guy was very advantageous. Elmer was more rational about negotiating for what made more sense in terms of business success, and he was less emotional than the doctors. He did not see any issue with kindly asking Julius to give them an extra month so that they could prepare for the move.

Elmer used emotion whenever he wanted, though. He made the call to Julius while the others listened in. He told the banker that although they appreciated the offer and wanted to sign, they could definitely use an extra thirty days so they could transition better. After all, Elmer underlined, trying to sell his point, uprooting whole families took much more time than two months. He also pointed out to Julius that for banks to ascertain a positive return on their investment, it was imperative that those institutions create an environment conducive to the success of those they loaned to.

Julius agreed to the extension. The doctors were very impressed with Elmer's tactful negotiation skills and were happy to have a different perspective on doing business, as medical school had not taught them business skills.

At that point, the pressure started to increase. The three stooges, as they fondly called themselves, started to plan the next step of meeting the contract lawyers. As a matter of principle, they all had their attorneys look through the contract, but they also had a corporate attorney look over the African partnership laws. Ownership was split into three thirds. It was also agreed that bylaws and a board of directors be created

The process was started by lawyers on the ground in Ghana, and the initial incorporation of the company went forward without a hinge. The fact that they had a great relationship with the banks streamlined the process and made it easier to negotiate the African bureaucracy, which, otherwise, would have been too time-consuming. The three partners were given updates on a daily basis as they started to tie up loose ends in America.

Of the three partners, the one having the most difficult time in the process of moving to Africa was Dr. Michael, as he was in the middle of a divorce. This was complicated by extreme illness of Lydia. Although they were separated, it was still very difficult for him to see the tough situation his wife was going through. In addition to her addiction to alcohol, the fact that Dr. Michael had filed for a divorce made her depression worse. Her family did not provide any help, and the relationship had soured a long time ago. Her siblings thought she had always looked down on her family and where she'd come from ever since she'd married Dr. Michael.

In Lydia's opinion, they were jealous of her success; she used to say that none of her childhood friends and family members had left their childhood town, that all her girlfriends had gotten pregnant in high school and those who were not junkies still lived in deplorable conditions. Her friends thought that she'd forgotten where she came from and shouldn't look down her nose at those who had made the wrong choices in life or hadn't been blessed with her luck.

As far as her children were concerned, they all knew that their mother had abused the financial privileges afforded to her by their father's hard work. The kids knew that their mother was not willing to seek help for her addiction. The fact that their father had been so patient for so long made the kids respect him even more; however, their relationship with their mother was severely strained, to the point where none of the kids would come home for special holidays like Christmas and thanksgiving. This exacerbated Lydia's depression. It was apparent that Lydia needed help but didn't know where to get it.

As Dr. Michael was getting ready to prepare for the move to set up the new business in Ghana, as a courtesy, he needed to let Lydia know what was going on, but he didn't know how she was going to take the news. She did not want the divorce, and perhaps she was hoping that things could clear up with the separation and they might be able to salvage the marriage. But she needed to understand that she was the reason why the family was getting broken up, not only her addiction but her unwillingness to seek help. He had already spoken with his kids and told them the news. They were fully aware that their parents were in the process of a divorce, which was not a surprise to them, knowing the issues with their mom. Their father was more than willing to keep the family together if Lydia was able to change her ways. The kids pleaded with their mom, but she was unwilling, so Dr.

Michael had no other choice, and luckily, his kids understood his predicament.

At around 11:30 pm on a Saturday night, Dr. Michael received a phone call from the local police, who broke the most awful news: Lydia had been found dead. They told him to come to the house at once.

Dr. Michael was shocked and horrified. He rushed to the house, which was cordoned off with yellow tape. He identified himself as the husband of the deceased and said that although they were separated, they were still legally married. The police report indicated that at about 10:40 pm, the local precinct received a phone call from the next-door neighbor, who reported hearing a gunshot. The neighbor was an old friend of Lydia's, one of those wine-tasting members Lydia had since lost as a friend due to her addiction. The neighbor was particularly concerned about Lydia and used to call Dr. Michael about what was happening in the house. She knew how much difficulty Lydia was going through, but unfortunately, Lydia cut off friends and families alike.

The police report continued that once they arrived, there was no answer at the door and they had to break into the house to check on Lydia. The officers found the ghastly scene of Lydia's lifeless body on a couch in her living room. She had suffered a gunshot wound to the head, and blood was everywhere. There was an empty bottle of wine and a glass on the table. The body was taken to the local hospital, where the death was ruled a suicide.

Dr. Michael was devastated. As a doctor, he had seen many deaths, both expected and sudden, but this one really hit home. He started thinking of what could have been, and he blamed himself. He thought that perhaps he could have tried harder to convince Lydia to check into a substance abuse treatment center. The first person he called to share the awful news was Dr. Khalid, with whom he had developed a close friendship. Dr. Khalid told him that he should not be too hard on himself, that God's will was at play and people can only be helped when they are willing.

Dr. Khalid's advice was a great relief for Dr. Michael, and it helped him turn the next page and inform his kids and Lydia's family of the tragic event. He had to arrange a conference call with his four kids, who were residing in three different time zones. He told them what happened and the plan for their mother's funeral. It was one of the worst phone calls he had ever made.

Lydia's funeral brought the entire Michael family home. Though the homecoming was sad, it was an opportunity to get everyone together.

The partnership business plan to create a healthcare company in Ghana took off in earnest. During the first Zoom meeting, the owners discussed things with incorporation lawyers and were informed that all

their ducks were in a row and all legal entities had been created according to the laws and regulations of the Accra Chamber of Commerce. The partnership was agreed upon. Elmer was to be the first to move to Ghana, as the doctors had to remain to close their businesses and transition smoothly from their affiliated hospitals in the US.

# 7

# LIFE IN A NEW WORLD

*I believe in Liberty for all men: the space to stretch their arms and their souls, the right to breathe and the right to vote, the freedom to choose their friends, enjoy the sunshine, and ride on the railroads, un-cursed by color; thinking, dreaming, working as they will in a kingdom of beauty and love."* **W. E. B. Du Bois**

After returning from the US for a final time, Sabrina assumed her post as the African correspondent for the BBC. Her parents were extremely supportive of their baby daughter and looked forward to visiting her in the future. Lisa and Chad wanted her to consider a job with the *Washington Post*, where Chad's friend was chief of human resources, but Sabrina wanted to do things her own way. She could not bear the thought of her sister claiming the favor; plus, she wanted to give Africa a chance. Lisa finally came around after realizing that Sabrina was not going to change her mind; everyone wished her well.

Jibril was very helpful and helped Sabrina settle into her position very seamlessly. The whole group created a mini support group, and

Nikki, Justice, and other Americans who had settled in Accra welcomed the newcomers and sorted out any issues for them.

The story also got around that Dr. Khalid, Dr. Michael, and Elmer were on their way to Africa to set up a new company. Everyone was excited that what had once been a long-shot dream was beginning to bear fruit. The most excited of all was Nikki, who had started the project and put lots of work into it.

Elmer arrived in Accra to initialize the project and present the company's blueprint to real estate agents who were to identify a location for the main office, where the health care business was to be housed before clinics could be started. The commercial bank financing the loan had a real estate connection that made the process very smooth. The lease agreement for the building was finalized. The next step was to hire a marketing and public relations firm that could be tasked with introducing the new medical services that would be available for the citizens of Accra and its surrounding counties. As the preliminary fact-finding had shown, there was a great need for specialty doctors with quality and experience.

While the doctors were preparing to move, Elmer hired the nursing staff, receptionists, and care coordinators. Having Nikki there was so much help, as she knew many locals who wanted to transition into the new clinic. The schedule for the next six months was written in stone, so once the doctors arrived, they just hit the ground running. They received many referrals from other local clinics as well as regional hospitals. The exponential growth in terms of the number of patients as well as procedures performed necessitated that they hire new doctors and nurses. They even placed advertisements for American-trained doctors to join them, offering lucrative salaries and sign-on bonuses.

Jamal completed his first degree at a local university in Accra and decided to go to law school. His father practicing medicine there was a morale booster for the young man. The plan was for him to specialize in corporate law so that one day he could join the company that his father and his partners had created.

Sabrina and Jibril became more than colleagues and decided to get married after dating for a while. She planned an elaborate wedding and invited her family in the US. The entire American clan in Accra was invited to attend; it was like a homecoming party.

To honor and appreciate the work that Nikki had done to bring all those immigrants together, she was asked to speak at the wedding and highlight the success achieved by those who had dared to venture out of America to find a happier and healthier environment for themselves and their families. Nikki pointed out that it was never easy to leave the place one had called home for so long, but home was where one found happiness. She looked back on how she'd felt when she'd planned the move, the what-ifs and all the constant worries about how she was going to get along with the new culture and customs. She shared with the audience that every time she'd felt discouraged about leaving America for Africa, she had been faced with the unjust and constant violence against African Americans there. She did not want to raise kids in a place where they were going to be targeted for the color of their skin, where the police could shoot first and ask questions later.

She knew that the only battle she could not win was the one she was afraid of fighting, and not trying to live in Africa was akin to being afraid to fight a compulsory battle. She shared with the party attendees that she had never regretted making the decision to move to Africa for many reasons. Personally, she said, she felt lighter after leaving America, lighter from the pain of seeing discrimination and evil racism. Being with her own had transformed her gloomy and stressful existence into one of happiness and usefulness.

The fact that she had brought new and useful ideas to the

motherland both in health care delivery and social work made her feel that not only had she benefitted from the move, but she had also contributed to the new land: a win-win situation. She encouraged her friends and companions to continue to promote Africa to their friends back in the New World and to stress that Africa is the Next Big Thing.

DR. KASEY Y. FARAH